EVERNIGHT PUBLISHING ®

www.evernightpublishing.com

SAM CRESCENT

Copyright© 2021

Sam Crescent

Editor: Karyn White

Cover Art: Sour Cherry Designs

Jacket Design: Jay Aheer

ISBN: 978-0-3695-0304-6

SNAKE'S ADDICTION

DEDICATION

This is for all my readers. You're all amazing, wonderful, and supportive. I love hearing from all of you and you all make everything worthwhile. I hope you find Snake a great addition to the Chaos Bleeds crew.

SNAKE'S ADDICTION

SNAKE'S ADDICTION

Chaos Bleeds, 6

Sam Crescent

Copyright © 2015

Chapter One

"When's Devil getting back?" Snake asked, taking a sip of his whiskey. He turned back toward the bar seeing as the main door wasn't opening to show him Devil, the Chaos Bleeds club Prez, was back from his little escapade to Fort Wills. Alex had called him over a week ago to tell them what had happened with Tabitha, and now they were all waiting to see what was going on. None of them liked to think of Tabitha in the hospital. She was only a little girl, and no one messed with little girls as far as the Chaos Bleeds were concerned.

"I don't know. Why? You want to suck his dick?" Dick asked, taking a seat beside him.

"Shut the fuck up. I'm concerned," Snake said. "It's not every day you hear about a fucking four year old knocked unconscious."

"It's the world we live in, and it's fucked up." Dick opened a can of soda while Snake continued to drink his whiskey. Snake wasn't a recovering addict whereas Dick was. He didn't give a shit about drinking in front of Dick.

"We're all concerned. Regardless of the world no kid should have to see that," Ripper said, drying a glass behind the bar.

"Where's Judi?" Dick asked.

"She's up in my room, resting. I can't wait for this fucking baby to come. The wait is killing me."

"We've all got to wait." Snake take a sip of his drink, glancing back at the door. "You don't think it was some kind of ambush?"

"Fuck, man, Tabitha's been hurt. That's all we know," Ripper said.

"So why call Devil?" Snake asked looking at Dick then at Ripper. "The last time we were in town, Tiny wanted us out of it. Why call Devil now?"

"Because Devil has Simon," Dick said.

"What's that got to do with it?" Snake was getting tired of being left in the dark. He was jonesing for a fight. Ever since he'd gone to see *her* he'd been waiting for her to come back to him. He was getting sick and tired of always waiting for her. The New Year had come and gone, but still nothing from her.

He'd kissed her, and where was she?

"Where's who?" Mia asked, walking up behind him.

"What?" Snake asked.

"Dude, you totally said that shit out loud," Ripper said.

"What?" Snake wasn't getting on well right now.

"You said you'd kissed her and now what?" Mia said, leaning over to snag Dick's soda from the counter.

"Hey, I was drinking that," Dick said.

"Is this about that nurse? What was her name?" Mia asked.

"Jessica," Death said, walking up with Brianna.

His arm was slung over the girl's shoulders, pulling her in.

Snake didn't like this. He hated being the center of attention, and the way the guys were looking at him right now, it wasn't helping him any.

"This is the same nurse who you went on a date with?" Mia asked.

"Ripper," Judi said, coming downstairs.

All of them turned to watch as a heavily pregnant Judi came downstairs.

"Babe, what have I fucking told you?" Ripper dropped the glass he was using to run to Judi's side. His hand was on her stomach as he placed her arm around his neck.

"Something doesn't feel right."

"What do you mean it doesn't feel right?" Ripper asked.

"It hurts, Ripper. Look, my feet are swollen."

Standing away from the bar, Snake looked at Judi's feet to find they were swollen. She wore a lace nightdress that landed to her knees. Just one glance at her pale, sweaty face, and Snake knew in his gut something wasn't right. Her head lolled a bit as if she couldn't keep it upright.

"Are you okay? Baby, I need you to talk to me."

"I need to go to the hospital, Ripper. Something isn't right." Judi screamed suddenly, grabbing her stomach. "Ouch, it hurts. It hurts."

Snake didn't wait around for orders. Rushing out of the clubhouse, he jumped into the car as Ripper carried Judi out. Dick and Death were helping him.

"It's too soon. I can't give birth. It's too soon. Call Lexie." Judi stopped talking as a scream erupted from her.

"We'll do it." Ripper climbed in behind Judi.

"I've got you, baby."

Dick joined Snake in the passenger side. "The brothers will round up and meet us at the hospital."

Putting his foot to the gas, Snake went as fast as the car would let him. He needed to get Judi, the club princess, to the hospital.

She kept screaming and panting.

"I've got you, baby. I've got you. We're going to get through this. I promise you. Just breathe."

Pulling into the hospital, Snake was shocked to see Jessica making her way out of the hospital. She was carrying a helmet, and he didn't think. Honking the horn he grabbed her attention.

Climbing out, he opened up Ripper's door.

"Snake? What is it?" she asked.

"Judi. She's going into labor or something. We don't know what to do."

Jessica was already running toward him. She shoved her helmet at him, pushing Ripper out of the way. "Judi, do you hear me?"

"It hurts."

"I know. Tell me what's the problem."

"My feet hurt, and it feels like it wants to come out." Judi was panting with each breath she took.

"No, we're going to remain calm. Remember the deep breaths. Take deep breaths. Listen to my voice, and don't you dare let this little monster win now. You let it win and they'll have you wrapped around its little finger. Do you understand?" Jessica asked. "I'll be right back." She pulled away from the car. "Keep her calm."

"What do you think it is?"

"First birth, the swelling feet, the pain. I'd say pre-eclampsia. We'll need to do tests to confirm."

"Is it bad?" Ripper asked.

Jessica closed her lips, shaking her head. "I'll

grab a bed."

She made to run inside. Snake joined her. "It's bad, isn't it?"

"Yes, some women, if not treated, can die from it. It's like their body can't handle the baby. You were right to bring her." Together they pushed a spare bed while Jessica started shouting out orders to the other nurses. He got that she asked for a doctor, but that was about it.

Watching her, Snake admired her skill. She wasn't shaking but in control. Ripper and Dick were waiting, and they helped Judi onto a bed.

"Okay, Judi. Everything is going to be okay now. You're at the hospital, and we're going to do everything to make sure your little monster stays right where you need him or her to be." Jessica leaned in close, smiling at Judi. "I call him a little monster with affection. My brother, he always called me that."

"I'm not going to sue you for bad bed language, Jess," Judi said.

"Good 'cause I'd have to kick your ass, and I'm against kicking pregnant women's asses."

Judi started to chuckle.

They pushed her into the hospital where there was already a small team waiting. A man in a white coat moved forward. "Tell me what I've got, beautiful."

Snake didn't like him one bit. He stayed back while Jessica gave the doctor a rundown of Judi's status. When it was over, she turned back toward him. Her long raven hair was tied at the back, knotted around.

"I've got to go. She's in good hands. Ripper, follow me."

He watched as his brother walked beside the good doctor. Dick stayed with him. "I guess we're on a vigil for now."

"Should we call Devil?"

"We can call Devil but talk to *him*. You don't want Lexie to find out. It'll worry her." Dick slapped him on the back. "I'll get us some coffee."

Walking back outside, Snake put a call through to Devil. He had to call a second and a third time before he answered the call.

"You better have a good fucking reason for waking me up."

"Judi's in the hospital."

"Wait, what?"

"She's in the hospital with a suspected pre-eclampsia. We're on a vigil, and Ripper's with her. I just thought you should know."

"Shit, we'll try and get back tonight. Tabitha has only just woken up, but I'll get Simon to say his goodbyes in the morning. I can't leave my family behind."

"Don't worry. I'll keep you posted of her condition," Snake said. What else was he supposed to do?

"I can't tell Lexie. It could cause complications with her own pregnancy."

"I know. I'll keep you posted of everything that's happening. I promise I won't tell Lexie."

"Be honest with me, Snake. How does it look?"

"It doesn't look good. I was talking to Jessica, and some women … they die from this, Devil."

His Prez cursed over the line. "When are we ever going to get a fucking break? Judi's wanted this baby for a long time. She's waited to have time with Ripper. I'll get there as soon as I can."

He heard Devil's upset but then, Snake wasn't feeling all that great either. Judi meant a great deal to the club. All of them had been there when they saved her from a fucking pimp beating the shit out of her.

"There's nothing we can do."

"There is. Keep me posted, and I'll be there when I can."

Saying his goodbyes he walked back into the hospital. While he'd been on the phone, Curse, Death, Spider, Slash, Butler, and Pussy were waiting. Several of the guys would stay behind at the clubhouse to protect their shit. Mia, Sasha, and Brianna were also waiting. None of the club whores were present as they weren't allowed in club business.

Dick finished giving them an update, taking a coffee to him once he was done.

"You're offering me a coffee?"

"We were here first. They can get their own fucking coffee." Dick blew across the surface.

"What is it?"

"Wishing it was something a lot fucking stronger."

"If you loved the drink and drugs so much, why quit?"

"And leave the club? Believe it or not, Snake, I happen to love this fucking club. I loved it way more than any drink or drugs."

Snake shrugged. There wasn't anything else he liked more than the club. He kept his gaze on the door where Jessica had disappeared. His whole life he'd been used to women obsessing over him. This was new for him. He'd never obsessed about another woman or taken the time to get to know her.

What was it about the raven-haired nurse that had gotten under his skin?

****

"We'll monitor her and try to keep her BP under control. Poor girl," Dr. John Milford said.

Jessica nodded. "They brought her in just in

time."

"That they did." John turned toward her, smiling. "Shouldn't you have left?"

"I was leaving as they came. Well, there's nothing you can do now. Go ahead." He squeezed her arm before running his hand up and down. "Go and rest. I'll take care of her.

"Okay. I'm out. I'll update the family."

"They're bikers, Jessica. Not family."

"If you want a riot on your hands, you're going the right way about it. They'll cause some problems if you treat them like anything other than family."

"How do you know them?" he asked.

"I don't. I've heard about them, same as everyone else."

"You'll do good to steer clear of them."

Jessica hated being told what to do, especially by someone who was stereotyping the whole biker image. "I'll do what I think is necessary. Good night." She walked away before she did something she'd regret later. Milford was an asshole of the highest order. A great doctor but an asshole. He believed the nurses were his personal harem, and unfortunately several nurses had fallen for his charm. Jessica saw through him. She saw through all of his charm and bullshit, just like she'd seen through Snake's. The biggest problem was that kiss. Of all the things she anticipated from Snake it wasn't a flyby kiss on Christmas Eve. It had confused her. Lydia, her friend, didn't have the first clue about him being a man whore in the beginning. If she did, she was pretending that she didn't know. Her friend was a little strange when it came to relationships. There were two reasons that kept Jessica well away from Snake. Her first reason was her loyalty to her friend. Lydia was her friend and still had a thing for Snake. The second reason? She couldn't trust him. He was surrounded by pussy, and she'd never been the kind of woman to go hunting for pain.

Even to this day Lydia thought Snake was going to call her back. Snake was not the kind to call or to be nice. He was an asshole to the core just like Milford.

She made her way out toward the main reception, and as she stood at the door that separated her from the group, she took in the worried sight. They were a rough and tough biker club, but their love for the girl upstairs was clear to see to anyone.

Taking a deep breath, she walked toward them. Snake spotted her first, and he stood up. She was surprised to see he still held onto her bag and helmet.

"Hello," she said to all of them. She didn't look at Snake, didn't want to.

"What's the news?"

She didn't know who asked the question. Snake had gotten close to her, almost touching her shoulder he was so close.

"Judi's stable at the moment. We're keeping her monitored, and she's doing okay. I'm not going to lie, it could go bad, but we're here to make sure nothing bad happens."

They all thanked her, and she turned to Snake. "Can I have my helmet and bag?"

"I'll follow you out."

Jessica wasn't in the mood to argue. It was past two in the morning, and all she wanted to do was go home and go to bed. The moment they left the hospital she was hit by the cold late January air. She quickly pulled her jacket around her, trying to fight off the sudden chill.

"Thank you for helping me out there."

"I'm a nurse, Snake. I'd do it for anyone." She stopped at her bike and turned to him. "Can I have my helmet and bag back?"

"Why haven't you been by?"

"By?"

"Yeah, the club. Why haven't you been by the club to spend some time?"

She frowned. "I didn't know I had to come back."

"I kissed you."

"So?"

Jessica was confused. She pulled the bag he handed to her over her shoulder.

"So, you were supposed to come to the club."

He held her helmet captive, refusing to give it to her. She went to take it, and he moved it out of the way. "Very mature, Snake."

"Why didn't you come?"

"Well, I didn't invite you to kiss me, and I didn't know I was expected to come to you because of one stupid kiss."

"You thought the kiss was stupid?"

"God, Snake. What are you twelve? It was a damned kiss. One I didn't ask for and one you shouldn't have given." She made to reach for the helmet. He moved it out of her grasp, angering her. "You're just a child." She spat the words out.

"And you're a cold heartless bitch."

"What about Lydia, huh? You think I just want to be another one of the women you fuck?" She shoved him hard in the chest. "I don't know you. I've no intention of getting to know you. Back the fuck off." She shoved him a little more.

Snake wrapped his arm around her waist, dragging her up against him. The helmet he held rubbed against her ass.

"What the hell are you doing?"

"Showing you it was more than a stupid kiss."

Before she had the chance to protest, his lips were on hers.

At first Jessica started to fight, to kick and hit out at him. When his tongue ran over her bottom lip, she lost all the fight. He plundered her mouth, sinking his fingers into her hair. She gasped, and he took advantage by deepening the kiss.

The helmet was forgotten, and she heard it fall to the ground with a thunk. She didn't have time to think about her helmet. His large hand covered her ass, gripping her tightly.

She kissed him back, unable to control the deep yearning that was washing over her. He held her tightly to him, rubbing his cock against her. The nurse's scrubs she wore didn't hide his arousal. He was rock hard, pressing against her.

Snake broke away from the kiss. His lips teasing back to her ear. "I bet if I was to put my hand against your pussy you'd be soaking wet."

She tensed up, no longer wanting him touching her or anywhere near her. "And there you went and ruined it." She kneed him in the balls, angry that he'd ruined a perfectly reasonable kiss. "That was a stupid kiss as well. You're going to learn to keep your hands and lips to yourself, Snake. I don't want them. I never want them."

Bending down, she grabbed the helmet, placing it on her head. Straddling her bike, she didn't pay him any attention as she left the hospital parking lot. Jessica was angry at herself and angry at Snake for knowing that her pussy was indeed soaking wet. What kind of friend was she that she couldn't stop her body from responding to him? He was a man whore, the worst kind. Ever since Lydia fucked him, it was all Jessica had heard about. Snake this and Snake that. She was tired of hearing about the blasted man. Now he was kissing her, confusing her, and fucking insulting her.

No, she wouldn't be giving in to the horrid man.

She parked up outside of her home. Pressing a button, she waited for the garage doors to open. Placing her pride and joy against her shit car, Jessica locked up the garage before heading inside.

Living alone had its perks. She didn't have to worry about the time she kept, which meant extra shifts at the hospital. There was currently no man in her life, and she didn't have to worry about keeping her legs shaved all the time.

Closing up the downstairs, she made herself a hot chocolate before going upstairs to her bathroom. She lived in a two bedroom home that she had a mortgage on. At twenty-nine years old, she was happy with the way her life was going. No stress, no chaos, and no bikers.

Running herself a bath, she placed her cup on the edge of the bath near the taps. Staring at her reflection in the mirror she saw the dark patches under her eyes. Sleep would take them away, but they'd be back again tomorrow. Her life had become nothing but work. She loved her work, and it was now her life.

Pulling the band from her hair, she fingered out the length of hair. Not a single grey in sight. She'd not been with a man for a long time, so long. It had to be at least a year since she last had the pleasure of a living, breathing man. She owned a vibrator, but the experience was pitiful in comparison.

"You don't need Snake. You don't want Snake. He's not going to rock your world but cause problems." Expelling a breath that made her lips pucker, she shook her head.

Later that night it was Snake's name she called out when she found a less than satisfactory relief.

Chapter Two

After heading home for a shower, shave, and a bite to eat, Snake arrived back at the hospital to relieve Dick. It was early the next morning with no change in Judi's condition. Looking around the room he saw how hopeless they all felt. None of them could do anything to help her or Ripper. The other brother was just about to leave when Devil burst through the door, Lexie and the kids following close behind him. Devil's presence surprised Snake. He must have gotten up early enough for the kids to say goodbye.

"Where is she?" Devil asked.

"Prez, you got here fast."

"They didn't need us at Fort Wills any longer. Come on, I'm going to go and find my daughter." He took Josh off Lexie, and the family started toward the main desk. There was no sign of Jessica, and Snake was pissed.

The little bitch had kneed him in the nuts last night and left him lying in the snow. Not that he didn't deserve it. He'd taken things a little too far last night. He needed to learn to take his time.

"I'm heading out. Call if anything changes. Devil's on the case now, so we don't have to be," Dick said.

"I'm sticking around. I want to keep an eye on things." Snake slapped Dick on the back, heading back to the main reception area.

Several of the brothers were waiting around. Some of them were playing on their cell phones, and Snake noticed several of the patients walking through the door trying to be as far from them as possible.

"Anyone would think we got some disease or some shit," Snake said.

"Nah, they're just afraid we might fuck their wives," Butler said, smirking.

"You're still awake."

"I'm still awake and here waiting for the news. It'll kill Ripper if anything happens to Judi."

"It'll kill all of us, man. Judi's ours. She's club property."

Butler nodded. "I know, but it's different for us."

"Why? 'cause we don't have our dick inside her?" Snake winced, holding his hand up. "Shit, sorry, lack of sleep and I'm turning into a fucking monster."

"We don't fuck Judi, but Ripper's in love with her. We all love her. She means something to all of us, but we're not in love with her. Kind of like Devil, if he ever lost Lexie. It would hit us all hard, but it would kill Devil."

"Nah, nothing would ever affect the Prez."

"Then you're an idiot," Butler said. "Prez would kill himself to follow Lexie. I remember the way he was when she was pregnant with Elizabeth and then Josh. He was so scared of losing her. It tore him up. Devil will die for her."

Snake sat back thinking about the time Lexie was pregnant. It was hard on all of the club but especially for Devil. "Yeah, I guess you're right."

"I know I'm right." Butler stretched his legs out, locking his fingers behind his head. His shirt rode up showing the scars of his past drug taking.

"Do you ever miss it?" Snake had taken drugs in the early days of riding. He never liked waking up not knowing what he'd gotten into. Waking up next to a dead woman hadn't helped him. The woman had died of an overdose over fifteen years ago. It had shaken him up so much, he never touched drugs again. He liked a drink, not drugs.

"I'd be lying if I said no. I sometimes think it would be easier to just start up. I wouldn't remember shit like this. This is the hardest thing ever. Watching the people you care about suffer. Judi's suffered enough, and yet here we are. It's their first kid." Butler stopped talking, and Snake saw his jaw clench. "This is what I hate the most. Waiting, watching, seeing others try to fight falling apart. It's scary shit, man. What about you?"

"No, I don't miss the drugs. It has been so fucking long since I took anything, I can't even remember the high."

"You've found your high in other ways, Snake."

"I have?"

"Yeah, the fights you get into. Drinking. That cute little nurse you're chasing around."

"I'm not chasing a cute little nurse." Snake tensed up, looking toward the main doors. When did she work again? The little bitch owed him for the bruised balls.

"No? You're always looking toward the door. Last night, you were waiting for her, holding her helmet like a lovesick puppy. Face it, Snake. You've got a thing. The chase of her is giving you a high."

"She kneed me in the nuts."

"Conquering her would be a delight for you then." Butler slapped his thigh. "I've got to take a piss."

Shaking his head, Snake grunted out, turning back to look at some of his other brothers. None of them paid any attention to him. Leaving the hospital, he pulled out his smokes. It was freezing cold, and he zipped up his leather jacket. He couldn't be in there, not yet.

Inhaling on his cigarette, he looked toward the parking lot in time to see a car he remembered. Jessica parked toward the back of the parking lot just as the doctor from last night made an appearance. Snake couldn't recall the doctor leaving. He watched as the bastard parked next to his little bitch.

Snake couldn't look away even though he wanted to. Gritting his teeth, he waited as they walked toward the main doors.

"Maybe we could grab that coffee," bastard said.

"I don't think—"

"One coffee today at lunch. I'm not asking for much." The doctor kept talking even though Jessica looked to be trying to get out of it. She didn't want him.

"Hey, babe, it's about time you turned up," Snake said. He dropped his smoke to the ground, stubbing it out. Closing the distance between him and Jessica, he gripped the back of her neck, tugging her close.

"You need to pick that up," the doctor said, pointing to the cigarette on the ground.

Glaring at him, Snake tugged Jessica close. "What about that coffee today at lunch? I'm waiting around anyway."

"No news on Judi?"

"Devil's up with her now."

"Jessica, are you coming?"

"I'll be there in a moment, Milford."

Snake waited, keeping hold of the back of her neck. "You can take your hands off me now."

"I don't think so. You're being rather compliant, and I like that."

"You're an ass."

"So, we're doing lunch?"

"No, we don't have to do lunch."

Snake turned her so she didn't have a choice but to look at him. "What about Doctor Bastard?"

"Doctor Bastard?"

"Yep, I don't care to know his name. He's going to see you alone at lunch. Why don't you want to have a coffee with the loser anyway?"

"He's going through the nurses, and I'm a nurse. It seems he's deciding to add me to his list of the conquered."

Snake didn't like the bastard even more. "We're having coffee then. He'll catch you out or step it up."

"Why are you helping me?"

"Why not?"

"You're not the kind of man to give a woman a helping hand."

"You really have a low opinion about me, don't you?"

"I work with what I know, and I don't know anything great about you." She shrugged. "Will you let go of my neck now?"

"No, I like holding your neck. You'll do as you're told." He caressed the sides of her neck, enjoying the way she squirmed.

"You're annoying me, Snake."

"Lunch?"

"Fine. Lunch, but you keep your hands and lips to yourself."

"I won't come near you at all." He held his hands up, releasing her.

She glared at him before turning away to enter the hospital. Butler might actually be right. There was something thrilling about chasing after the doctor. She wasn't giving him anything, and he was having to fight for the smallest moments with her.

Taking a seat beside Butler, he saw the brother was smiling.

"What are you smiling about?"

"I could ask you the same question."

Shaking his head, Snake leaned forward, resting his elbows on his knees.

"Devil, Ripper, Curse, Pussy, Death, and now

you," Butler said, smirking.

"What the fuck are you talking about now?" Snake asked.

"Six brothers down. Wow, we're going to be a club filled with pussy." Butler couldn't stop laughing.

Listening to his brother laugh, Snake tried to ignore him. He wasn't falling for Jessica. There was nothing to his interest other than sex. He didn't want to get involved, have kids, or share their life together. A simple fuck was all he wanted, and he'd be happy with that.

Devil came down looking older than when he went up. Getting to his feet, all of the brothers gathered around.

"What's going on?" Spider asked, speaking up from the back.

"They're injecting her with steroids, preparing for a possible C-section. They can't keep her blood pressure down, and it's bad, boys. It's really fucking bad. Ripper's going to need you."

"I'll head out to the house and pick some shit up for them," Snake said.

"Butler, will you take the kids to Vincent? He knows what's going on and is keeping an eye on everything. Where's Pussy?"

"He's back at the clubhouse. Sasha's got the flu, and he's taking care of her."

"Okay, get Death to handle the decorators for the strip club. I want that up and running by February at the latest," Devil said.

"Prez, none of us care about the money. Judi needs to survive this," Curse said.

They all agreed. The strip club and the income it would make could wait. One of their own was down. They needed to focus on Judi getting well and being there for Ripper when he needed them most. They were all a family. If they lost her, Ripper was gone as well. They would all mourn Judi's loss.

****

Jessica finished binding up the arm of a five-year-old who'd fallen downstairs from all the excitement. Tansy was helping Milford with Judi. She didn't know what was going on with Judi. It shouldn't bother her, but it did. Giving the instructions on caring for the arm to the child's mother, she saw them out of the room, giving them directions on where to go. When it was finished, she wrote up the chart taking it through to the main reception. The Chaos Bleeds crew was still waiting. She didn't see any signs of Snake. Grabbing another chart, she called one of the women through.

"I don't like them being in the hospital," the woman said.

"Please take a seat on the bed." Glancing through the chart, Jessica saw she was having some abdominal pain. She asked the necessary questions, pressed lightly on her stomach. "I'm going to take you for an x-ray."

"Is it serious?"

"I'll see what the x-rays tell me."

"No, not about me. I'm talking about those bikers being here. I'd love to know."

Gossiping townsfolk pissed Jessica off more than anything. "I can't disclose as to why they're here."

"Biker groups are so bad and dangerous. Have you seen the women who hang around them? They're sluts, all of them. I wouldn't dream of being near them even in my day when I was a looker."

Rolling her eyes, Jessica helped the woman into a wheelchair.

My job is to care.

Jessica listened as the woman kept on talking

about everything she hated about bikers and how they were bringing the town of Piston County down.

Jessica bit her lip, going behind the protective shield while the x-ray was happening.

"You've got a talkative one today, Jess," Malcolm, the guy who took the pictures, said.

"She hates bikers."

"I feel sorry for them," Malcolm said. "I heard one of their women was inside. Pre-eclampsia?"

"Yeah, I know." Jessica signed some forms, putting her pen back into her uniform.

"They're in here, and they've got women like her making it hard. From what I know, they pay their taxes and keep to themselves."

Jessica had heard a lot more than that but kept her mouth shut.

"Thank you, Malcolm."

The woman had wind built up, which was causing her pain. She got the doctor, Milford, to sign off on some laxatives, and rest.

"So, how about that coffee?"

"I'm having coffee with Snake. Sorry," she said, glancing down at her watch.

"You should really think about who you associate with," Milford said.

"And why is that?"

"The reputation of this hospital for one."

Cocking her head to the side, Jessica stared at Milford. "Look, I can have a coffee with whoever I want just like you can choose to screw who you want to. Back off, Milford. You're not getting into my pants."

He raised a brow. "Are you going to threaten me with sexual harassment?"

"No. You're not harassing me, but I can make your life just as uncomfortable as you can make mine.

Think about that, Milford." Turning on her heel, she gave the woman a prescription then made her way out to the reception room. Snake was waiting for her. He was surrounded by several brothers.

Taking a deep breath, she walked over to him. "Coffee?"

"You've decided to have one with me now?"

"Please, Snake. I'm not in the mood."

"You said please?"

"So, come on. Coffee." She didn't stand around waiting for him. Behind her, she heard several catcalls follow him.

"Where's the lunch room?"

"Upstairs off the child's ward." She took the stairs, not wanting to be alone with him in the elevator. When Snake crowded her, she didn't seem to be able to keep any focus on herself. Walking up the steps, she was aware of his presence on the way up behind her.

Biting her lip, she tried not to wonder if her ass looked big or not.

"You don't have to crowd behind me," she said.

"I like looking at your ass. Deal with it."

In no time at all they were in the lunch room. She spotted Milford in the corner with Bernie, another nurse, slender with blonde hair.

Expelling a relieved breath, Jessica grabbed a tray. "Pick what you want and I'll pay."

"I can pay for my own stuff."

"I know, but you're doing this as a favor to me. I owe you." She took a tray of lasagna that looked way too over-cooked, a large slice of chocolate cheesecake, then ordered a strong black coffee.

Snake had two burgers and fries, two cheesecakes, a large cookie, and a milkshake.

She paid the woman serving on the till before

finding a table. Keeping her back to Milford, she focused on the man in front of her. Snake sat his large body down. She couldn't help but look away from the thickness of his arms. Did he work out? His muscles looked hard and defined. They were not covered in ink either. He did have patterns on his arms but nothing that would cover his arms.

"Doctor Bastard keeps looking over at you."

"He threatened me before I came here. He warned me that I should think about the kind of people I hang out with."

"And yet you're here with me."

"I don't like being ordered around."

"You don't like authority?"

"No, I don't. I used to piss my dad off all the time, and my brother. They believe I was always looking for trouble."

"Where are your parents?"

"They live in the city. My father's a lawyer, brother is a doctor. Mother is a housewife. You?"

"I don't have any parents, and I'm not going to talk about them."

"Oh, sorry."

"Don't be. I'm not."

She couldn't look away as he took a large bite of his burger. His hands were so large and powerful looking. Taking a bite of her lasagna she tried not to wince at the overly herbed food.

"This is shit, you know that right?" Snake asked, swallowing.

"What?"

"The food. This burger was cooked in the eighteen hundreds. It had to be, it was that fucking disgusting."

Against her better judgment she started to laugh.

Once she started she couldn't stop. It had been so long since she'd found anything funny.

"You'll owe me another date. You liked our other date."

The laughter stopped instantly.

"I don't know about that, Snake."

"You've got a problem being with me?"

Licking her lips, she pushed the pasta away from the sauce. "I've not got a problem with you."

"Then what have you got a problem with?" he asked. "Lydia?"

"She's my friend."

"Your friend is a little freak. She kept trying to slap me and make me her bitch. I wouldn't fuck her again even if my life depended on it."

Jessica didn't want to think about her friend and her sudden interest in BDSM. She knew Lydia was reading books and watching videos online, but to actually slap someone? Lydia didn't strike her as a slapper, but then, she didn't want to know anything about her friend's sex life. She should have known though. Who dates a guy who goes by the name Master?

"I, erm, I don't know what to say about that."

"How are you and Lydia friends? She's a freak and works—I don't know where she works?"

Chuckling, she stared at Snake. Last night she'd come screaming his name, and now she was eating her lunch with him.

"I don't know what you want from me?"

"I want you to give me a chance."

"You fuck women and forget about them." Jessica pushed her lasagna aside, no longer wanting the food. Instead, she decided to eat the cheesecake.

"Do you believe in love and soul-mates?"

"No, I don't."

"Do you believe in fun?"

"Snake, I appreciate you having dinner with me. I do, but this isn't going to go anywhere."

"What is Lydia up to now? Is she still pining after me?"

At Christmas all Lydia had talked about was Snake. Now, she had a new man in her life. Jessica didn't know his name, but she always called him Master. It was a strange thing, but Jessica wasn't interested in coming between her friend and happiness.

"I don't think she's pining after you. She's moved on. I think." It had been a week since she last heard from Lydia. Jessica was an awful friend. When she finished lunch she'd call Lydia.

"Then give me a chance."

"Can we change the subject?" She didn't want to give into him. Yes, she believed in fun, but with Snake? She didn't want to get involved with him.

"I will get past that little wall you've built up, Jessica."

She didn't say anything. They ate their lunch talking about Judi and what could happen. When it was over, Jessica was sad to see Snake leave.

Leaving the hospital, she dialed Lydia's number. It went straight to the answering machine.

"Hey, Lydia. I miss you. Please give me a call when you get this." Hanging up the phone, Jessica blew out a breath. This was turning out to be a long day.

****

"Wait, what do you mean?" Devil asked.

"We need to prepare her for an immediate C-section. The baby, it's in distress, and Judi's deteriorating. If we leave it too long I fear she will end up in a coma," Milford said.

Glancing through the window into the hospital

room, Devil saw Judi's pale face. She was resting against the pillows, but she was too weak to even hold the oxygen mask to her mouth.

"It's ten weeks too soon," Ripper said. "The baby could die?"

"We have a brilliant neonatal unit here. I promise you. Your child would be taken care of."

Devil looked toward Ripper. He saw the pain, the confusion, the fear all play across the man's face. This was not a decision he had to make.

"Is there a chance she'll just get better?" Ripper asked.

"There's a chance. It's very slim, and in her condition, it's unlikely. I can leave it another couple of hours—"

"What could happen in those couple of hours?" Devil said.

"Like I said, she could get worse."

They didn't have time for her to get worse. It was a fifty-fifty chance. Closing his eyes, he rubbed them, feeling years older than he actually was.

"I'll give you a moment to make a decision."

"Devil, I can't do this."

"She's your woman. Your life is lying in that bed. You've got a choice here, do the C-section or don't." Devil swallowed past the lump forming in his throat. "Neither of those choices gives you a great outcome. You could lose Judi or your kid, or both."

Ripper turned away, slamming his fist against the wall. "I can't do it. I can't lose them both, Devil."

"Then make a choice. This is your choice."

Devil knew what he'd do. He'd never risk his woman. Lexie knew, and hated him for it, that if it ever came down to a choice, save his baby or save his woman, he'd save her. They'd argued about it enough times.

"I can't lose her. I don't care about the kid if I don't have her."

"Then make the call." Devil contained his relief as he watched Ripper call the doctor back.

"Do the C-section. You save my woman, do you hear me?"

"We're going to have to do this now. Bernie, take this man and prepare him to be seated with his wife."

Devil pulled Lexie away from the crew as they worked on Judi. Their girl was fading, growing weaker because of the baby inside her.

"I get what you mean," Lexie said.

"What, baby?"

"I know I'm not much older than Judi, but she's ours. I wouldn't let Ripper kill her for the baby. I couldn't do it."

"Then you better stop arguing," he said. Kissing her head, he watched the nurses start to prepare Judi. He couldn't lose her now. She deserved to live a full life, one with kids.

Chapter Three

The whole of the hospital was tense as Devil had given them all the news. Judi was going in for a C-section. Snake's hands were shaking as he started to pace the hospital. It was past seven, and they hadn't heard any news.

"What happens to the baby?" Mia asked. "It's ten weeks early. This is going to break Judi's heart if anything happens to it."

They didn't know the sex of the baby as they wanted it to be a surprise.

"She'll get through this. She's strong." This came from Dick, who was sitting in the corner.

They were all tense as they waited to find out what was happening.

When he couldn't stand the silence, Snake left the hospital to have a smoke. The cold hit him, and once he stared up at the sky, he forgot all about the smokes.

"Have you heard any news?" Jessica asked.

Opening his eyes, he watched as the woman who refused to give him the time of day moved toward him. She held a large box in her arms.

"What are you doing?" he asked. She wasn't wearing her scrubs. Her hair was down, spilling around her in luscious waves.

"I didn't want you eating eighteenth century burgers. I went to the diner in town. I thought you could all eat something." The box looked heavy. Stepping forward, he made to relieve her from the box, but Jessica held it tightly. "Why are you here?"

"Bernie told me what was happening. On my way out I saw you all waiting." She wouldn't look at him. "Let me help you, Snake."

He wanted to get more out of her but decided

against it. Taking the box from her, they entered the hospital. When one of the women behind the reception desk tried to stop them from eating, the brothers silenced her with a look.

Snake watched as Jessica handed out burgers and coffee. Everything was wrapped up, and there was still heat coming from it. Once they handed everything out, she took a seat beside him. He took a bite, moaning at the succulent meat.

"You still owe me a date."

"Okay," she said, no longer arguing.

"You're confusing."

"Don't talk about it. I'm confusing myself right now. I promised myself that I'd stay away."

"Then why are you here?"

"Everyone needs to have a friend at a time like this."

"I'm surrounded by friends. I don't need you."

"Why are you always following me if you don't need me?" she asked, firing a question back at him. "We all need someone, Snake."

"You've made it clear that you don't need me."

The rest of the hospital fell away as he stared at her. She was the most beautiful woman he'd ever seen. Her raven hair fell down to her waist, and he could imagine wrapping the length around his fist as he fucked her hard. He would bet every cent to his name that she had a nice tight pussy, soaking wet as well. Her blue eyes held him captive. What he loved the most was when she licked at her bottom lip, driving him crazy.

"I want to be here."

She took hold of his hand, locking their fingers together. He didn't like the thrill that he got from her touch. No woman had him torn up like this. He was a Snake. He struck his prey when they least expected it.

He didn't pull away. Tightening his hold on her hand, they sat together and waited.

"You'll hear something soon," she said.

Twenty minutes passed before Devil came out. "She's alive," he said. "She's stable, and her blood pressure is coming down."

The whole club breathed a sigh of relief.

"What did she have?" Mia asked. "The baby?"

"He's in neonatal at the moment. Ripper said he came out screaming, but he's overworked himself. They've got him on oxygen, and they've hooked him up."

Snake didn't know what to say.

"You can all come and visit her, two at a time," Devil said.

"Wow, someone must have scared the doctor."

"Why?" Snake asked.

"Only close family is allowed to visit at a time like this."

"Look around you, Jessica. We're her closest family. No one is going to get rid of us."

"I can see that." She smiled.

"Snake, are you coming?" Devil asked.

"Go," Jessica said. "I'll be here when you get down. I won't run away."

Nodding, he released her hand, missing her touch the moment he did. He walked up with Dick. Curse and Mia were before him.

"Has Ripper gone to see the baby?" Snake asked.

"No. He doesn't want to see him, not yet."

"This is going to be a long road for the little guy," Mia said.

"We're all here for them. This was a damned scare."

Sitting outside with Dick, they waited for Curse

and Mia to go through.

"Fuck me, that had to be the hardest couple of days," Dick said.

"It could still get worse." Snake leaned on his knees waiting for his turn to go and see Judi.

"Yeah, it could."

Neither of them spoke as nurses and doctors walked past. He listened to the quiet commotion of what was happening around him. Snake didn't like it; in fact he hated it.

Curse and Mia left, and Snake got to his feet going inside the room. Lexie was sitting on one side while Ripper sat on her other side as close as he could get to his wife.

"Hey," Judi said, smiling.

She looked weak, tired.

"Hey," Snake and Dick said at the same time.

"I'm so sorry for scaring you."

"What's going on now?" Snake asked, gripping the bars at the end of the bed.

"I'm waiting for the epidural to wear off. I can't feel my feet or legs. I'm numb from the waist down. I'm going to have a horrible scar." She stuck her bottom lip out. "I'm trying to convince Ripper to go and see our son."

"I'm not going anywhere without seeing you."

"Would you like me to go and see him?" Snake asked. "I could take Jessica. She could give me a rundown of all that shit. Take a photo if I'm allowed."

"Would you do that?" Judi asked, smiling. "I would really like to see him again."

"I'll go and do it now."

"Thank you."

Leaving the room, Snake went to grab Jessica. She was reading a book when he entered the waiting room.

"Are you done?"

"No, I need you to take me to the neonatal unit. Judi wants a picture of her kid."

"Snake, I don't think they allow—"

"I've gotten their permission. Judi needs to see her son. Please." He wasn't beyond begging for Judi.

"Okay, okay, I'll help." She got to her feet, taking his hand. They walked toward the doors. He moved behind her, following her. Ripper was exiting the room as they walked in.

"I thought you weren't going to see him," Snake said. The sound of screaming babies hit him hard.

"I can't see him, but I had to sign your names down. I'm going back to my woman." Ripper was gone before he could say anything more.

"It must be hard for him."

"I don't think it is. He's feeling guilty."

"How do you know?" Jessica asked.

"I know Ripper, and I know what he's feeling. At the moment he's angry at the baby for putting his woman at risk."

"But that's stupid," Jessica said.

"Is it? Judi's the love of Ripper's life. He risked everything for her, and now he almost lost her. Ripper can't go and see his kid until the anger goes." Snake signed himself into the room, nodding at the woman. The nurse showed them toward Ripper's kid. He was in an incubator, hooked up to a machine.

The sight made any anger Snake had disappear. This little guy was going to be loved by the whole club.

"How can anyone be angry at him?" Jessica asked.

"It's not directed at him," Snake said, trying to amend his earlier comment. "It's what he could have done." Pressing his fingers to the glass, he let out a breath. "He's so small."

"He's ten weeks early. It's going to be hard couple of weeks, if not months."

"Damn, I didn't think he'd be that small."

"What did you think? He'd be a grown assed man so you could beat him up for hurting Judi?"

"No, I didn't." He turned to look at Jessica. Tears were shining in her eyes. "What is it?"

"Nothing. I just, I hate seeing babies like this."

Snake didn't like the way he felt from witnessing her upset. Women crying usually pissed him off, and he wanted out of their lives. This wasn't the case with Jessica. Gripping the back of her neck, he pulled her close, pressing a kiss to her forehead. "It's okay."

"He's so little."

"Yeah, he is. He'll be big soon. Can I take a photo of him?" Snake asked. He didn't want to let go of her.

"Providing you don't get anyone else or other babies, you should be fine."

He pulled out his cell phone. Accessing the camera, he took several shots. His heart broke for the little baby hooked up to machines. When he was done, he took her hand, leading her away.

"Come with me. I just want to show Judi these shots."

They made their way out of the neonatal unit. "Do you think I should go up there?"

"Yes. You're coming with me."

He didn't let her go as they made their way up to her room. Spider and Dime were inside the room this time.

"I've got the pictures." He released Jessica long enough to hand Judi his phone.

****

"He's so beautiful," Judi said, smiling down at the phone. Jessica watched the young mother, wishing with all of her heart nothing went wrong. This was the one day where she left work early and now she was back because she couldn't stay away. Lydia wasn't answering her phone, and when she wasn't answering her phone, Jessica didn't know why she should steer clear of Snake.

"Take the phone," Snake said.

"Are you sure?"

"Yeah, you look at that little guy."

"Ripper, you've got to go and see him."

Jessica couldn't stay to watch anymore. It broke her heart. This was why she stayed with her emergency room, handling cases that were fleeting, not cases like Judi.

"Jessica, wait up!"

She kept walking, needing to get out in the fresh air. The brothers didn't look up as she made to pass them. Only Snake calling her name followed her. She grabbed keys out of her back pocket determined to get out of the hospital. There was no way she was going to fall for his tricks. She was done with this shit. She didn't want to fall for a biker, a man whore biker.

"Will you fucking stop?" He grabbed her arm, pressing her against her car.

"What are you doing?"

"Stopping you from getting yourself killed. You're not in the right frame of mood to drive." He took the keys from her fingers. "I'll drive you home."

"I can drive myself."

"I'm not going to let you."

He opened the door, helping her inside. Jessica no longer saw the point in fighting. He was only going to get what he wanted anyway.

Gritting her teeth, she watched as he readjusted her chair so that he was comfortable behind her wheel. She didn't like it, and she didn't like him.

You want him.

He was the first man in a long time that she actually wanted to fuck. The only reason she'd not been with someone in the last year was because she didn't want to.

"I know where you live."

"I remember." Resting her head on her hand, she stared out of the window. It was already dark, and she just wanted to head home. This was a half day for her, getting home before the next day.

She remembered his kiss so bad that it scared her. No one should ever have power over someone else with a single kiss.

"Are you going to explain what that was all about?"

"Nope. I don't like seeing kids like that or anything like that." She licked her lips.

"Have you ever had kids?"

"No. Never had kids or been married. I'm not the kind of person to settle down. I did have a steady thing going once with one man, and then I decided against it."

"Oh, yeah, what happened?"

"The guy was a cheating scumbag, and after I witnessed him in action I hated him. He fucked anything that walked. Remind you of someone?"

"I'm not offering you forever."

"You're not offering me anything other than a bad friendship."

"Lydia has nothing to do with this. That woman is weird. You don't need to hang out with her."

"What? Hang out with you instead? Maybe the women of the club?" Jessica snorted. "I don't think so.

I've no intention of being anything to you, Snake."

He pulled up outside of her house. Climbing out, she clicked the button on her garage, following him inside. He parked her car up alongside her bike. She loved her precious bike. It was the one thing she did love in this world.

"Thank you for driving me home."

"I could use a coffee. It's cold outside. I'm thirsty, and I've got to get back to the hospital."

"Fine, come on." She opened the door leading up to her house. Flicking the light off, she made sure the doors were all locked before heading toward her kitchen. Ignoring his presence was her safest option right now. She didn't trust herself to be with him or to be anything with him.

"Your house is nice," he said.

Staring at their reflections in the window, she quickly looked away. He was so tall and muscular. The sheer size of him made her place feel so small.

"Thank you."

Putting the kettle on, she stared down at her hands seeing them shake. What the hell was wrong with her?

Reaching for the cupboard, she gasped as Snake's hand wrapped around hers, holding her still.

"What are you doing?"

"I know what's wrong."

"Yeah?"

"Yeah. You want this, and that scares you. You're held by some sort of moral high code, and the truth is, you want me."

"My God, the ego." She turned around with him still holding her and wished she hadn't. He was close, so close that she wasn't able to look away from him. "What are you doing?"

"You're afraid that this will be more than fucking."

"I'm not going to fuck you."

"No?"

"No." She was fighting her own needs. Her pussy was slick, dripping, and all he was doing was touching her. When she thought the worst about him, it was easier, so damned easy. Seeing him vulnerable with the club made it hard for her. Snake felt a hell of a lot more than he let people believed. She'd seen that little baby, and she saw the love in Snake's eyes. It had her yearning for someone to look at her with such love and devotion. She'd given all of this up to become a nurse.

Jessica hated distractions, and men were only distractions to her.

"Baby, you're lying to yourself. Do you think Lydia would hold back right now? Do you think if it came down to a man you wanted, she'd hold back?"

She didn't like where this was going. "This is none of your business."

"No? I bet she'd be riding any cock she damn well liked. This friendship you've got yourself believing means something, is bullshit. You're the only one that feels it."

All along she'd known the truth, but she didn't want to believe it. "You've got to go."

The walls she'd built up were crumbling. She wanted Snake, not forever just for a moment. He pressed her hand against the cupboard, locking his fingers around her wrist. Stroking down her cheek, Jessica didn't fight him as he caressed across her chest. "Tell me to stop because you want me to stop. Don't push me away because of some stupid girl agreement between friends or because of what I was like before you. Take a chance."

Lydia would fuck anyone she wanted. There

wouldn't be a single concern to what Jessica wanted. Snake was right. The only person Lydia ever really cared about was herself. Jessica hated admitting the truth, but it was in fact the truth. Between her loyalty for Lydia and her reservations about Snake, she didn't know what else held her back. She wasn't looking for commitment, so why should his past bother her?

He'd gotten under her skin, and she couldn't move on until she had him. Her other hand was free. Reaching out, she stroked over his rock hard cock. Staring into his eyes, Jessica broke down the rest of her walls.

"What's it going to be, Jessica?"

"I've got my hand on your cock. What do you think it's going to be?"

"I'm not interested in a woman who'll scream rape afterwards." His voice got a little thicker as he spoke. Shoving her hand inside his jeans, she cupped him. There wasn't anything small about him. When he finally fucked her, ramming his cock inside her, it would hurt. He was large, larger than any man she'd been with.

"I don't cry rape. I'm not that kind of woman. I want this. You want this, and I'm tired of fighting it. You're right, Lydia would fuck you if I'd wanted you or not." She'd done it many times before in the past. Jessica never held it against her, but then, she rarely held anything against anyone. Snake was different. He was the first man she'd ever gotten angry over for Lydia.

For several seconds neither of them spoke or did anything. Snake stared at her, and she stared right back. He was used to getting what he wanted, and he wanted this. She wanted this as well. There was no way she could go another night of screaming his name in an unsatisfied climax.

The fingers on her chest began to unbutton the

shirt she wore. She still didn't look away, stroking his cock. He pushed her shirt aside, holding her hand above her head.

"Are you going to let me go?"

"No, I like having you pinned down. I'm going to need to look into some rope for my bed."

She smiled, crying out as he lowered his head to her chest. He sucked her nipple through the lace fabric of her bra. She wore a white bra with a matching pair of lace panties. Underwear was one of her greatest weaknesses.

He moved to her other breast, sucking the tip inside.

"Your tits are so large. They fill my hand perfectly. I want to watch them bounce in front of my face as I fuck you hard."

She reached around the back of his neck, gripping his hair, she tugged him down. He had to stop talking. He released her hand, wrapping both of his around her, trapping her against the counter and his hard body. His hands were everywhere, in her hair, running down her back. He didn't hold one part of her but kept touching everywhere. She couldn't focus, nor did she care.

She pulled away from his cock to tug at the belt of his jeans. At the same time, he shoved her jeans down her thighs. The rough fabric scraped along her skin in the process. She didn't care about the bite of pain. He lifted her up onto the counter as if she weighed nothing. Her legs were thrown open, and he yanked her panties off. His fingers glided through her core, and he slammed a finger inside her.

"You're so fucking wet, baby."

"Condom. You need a condom." She panted. The smallest touch of his finger and she was ready to go up in flames. He kicked off his jeans, reaching down into the back pocket. She watched as he threw at least four onto the table, while using the fifth to slide over his dick. She didn't want to think about why he had so many condoms.

Watching him work the latex over his cock turned her on. He still wore a shirt, and hers was open, revealing her chest.

"Don't you want any foreplay, baby?" he asked.

"No. I just want your dick inside me."

He aligned the tip to her entrance. She stared down seeing how big he was. In one jarring thrust, half of his dick was inside her. Jessica couldn't help but scream out. He was huge, and there wasn't any room for her to go.

Snake was making her very aware of the fact she'd not had sex in a long time.

Chapter Four

Jessica's pussy was the tightest he'd ever had the pleasure of fucking. Snake gritted his teeth as he held still inside her. She was having trouble accommodating him. His cock wasn't small. Reaching around, he grabbed her ass bringing her to the edge of the counter so that she was almost off it completely.

Slowly, he slid the last couple of inches inside her.

"Look at us, Jessica. Look at my dick."

She opened her eyes, which she'd closed when he started to fuck inside her. The moment she looked at them joined, her pussy squeezed him even tighter.

"Fuck, baby."

He started to press in and out of her, over and over again, little tiny thrusts so he could enjoy the flutters of her cunt. She held onto the counter, rolling her hips and fucking him.

"It's not enough. I need you to fuck me."

She'd wrapped her legs around him, and now she lowered them to the floor. He pulled out of her only to be surprised as she pushed him into a chair. Snake didn't get a chance to wait. She straddled his lap, gripping his cock as she pressed him inside her pussy. Jessica was the first woman to take the lead, to fuck him. The club whores did as he commanded. He either threw them to the bed or bent them over a surface close by, taking them from behind.

With club whores he didn't have to try. They were there for the club cock, nothing else.

Jessica cried out as she took the whole of his cock when she slammed onto him. Gripping her ass, he cursed. "You take it fucking easy." He didn't want to hurt her, and this was another surprise for him. There were plenty of women out there that he'd never given a fuck about what they did to themselves. Outside of the hospital watching her walk over the frozen ground without a care for her own safety had pissed him off. He didn't like the way he was behaving over her. There was something possessive in his need to be with her. She was plaguing his every thought.

"What's the matter, Snake? Never had a woman fuck you before?" She tugged on the hairs at the back of his neck, bouncing on his cock.

Thrusting up inside her, he held tightly to her ass. There would be bruising from the strength of his grip on her ass. "You want my cock? Take it all." He brought her down as he fucked up inside her. He gave it all to her, his strength, the length of his cock. She didn't back down, crying out, and digging her fingers into his shoulders.

"Please, I want to come."

He tugged her off his cock, placing her onto the round table. It wasn't overly large but enough. Turning in his chair, he sucked her clit into his mouth. She screamed out his name. Slamming two fingers inside her tight pussy, he turned them to stroke over her G-spot. She started to thrust up to his mouth. Pressing a hand to her stomach, he kept her on the table, making sure she didn't move. Flicking her clit, he slid down to replace his fingers with his tongue.

"Fuck, yes, fuck," she said, panting.

She was soaking wet, and her cum was the sweetest he'd ever tasted.

"Come for me, Jess." He stroked his thumb over her clit, fucking into her pussy. Within seconds she came apart screaming his name. He'd never forget the sound of his name on her lips.

Before she finished climaxing, he spun her around so she was bent over the table with her ass in the air. Running his hands over her rounded cheeks, he spread them open to get a look at her ass and pussy.

Without waiting, he fed his condom covered cock into her dripping pussy. Wrapping her raven hair around his fist, he tugged the length back so that she was drawn off the table. Slamming every inch of his dick into her, he held her there.

"I'm going to fuck you, baby. I want you to scream my name."

He wished there was a mirror so that he could see how fucking sexy she looked under his control. Slapping her ass, he drove into her hard. Landing blows to her ass cheeks with his hands, he fucked her hard, giving her every inch of his cock. He couldn't stop himself the moment he started.

She begged him for more, and he gave it to her. From the first moment they met at the hospital, through their date, and to now, this had been building. Neither of them could deny the attraction they both clearly had for each other. He didn't want to deny it. Snake needed to fuck her out of his head. He couldn't think about what it meant or what he wanted. This was sex. No woman would ever get anything out of him but sex.

The table started to move with the force of his thrusts. He wasn't going to last. Cursing, he slammed inside her twice more, filling the condom with his cum. It was the most explosive orgasm of his life. He felt utterly drained.

Taking deep breaths, he slowly released her hair, lowering her to the table. His cock was still twitching inside her pussy. The sounds surrounding them were those of their heavy breathing. Pulling out of her tight pussy, he hated it.

Jessica didn't stay there. She got to her feet, bending down to grab her jeans. He saw she was shaking.

What the hell had just happened?

"You can see yourself out?"

"Jess," he said, staring to speak her name. He didn't have a clue what to say.

"Lock up."

She didn't look back toward him. The kettle had long since boiled. He didn't want to leave this like this.

Watching her leave when she wasn't even looking at him, pissed him the fuck off. Why wasn't she looking at him?

Picking up his jeans, he pulled them up his body. The condom was still on his dick. Pulling it off, he tied it up, throwing it in the trash. He washed his hands, then for some reason, he cleaned off the table. Snake didn't do domestic shit, and yet he couldn't leave. He didn't have his cell phone on him as Judi had that because his phone had the pictures of her son, and he didn't want to call one of the brothers to pick him up. If someone needed him they'd come and find him. Enough of the crew had seen him running out to Jessica. It wouldn't take long for them to find him.

He made them both a coffee, looking through her cupboards to find the cups, spoons, milk, sugar, and coffee. With two cups in his hand, he walked toward the front door, checking to make sure it was locked. Once he was satisfied that it was all safe, he made his way upstairs.

Turn back.

This is complicated shit.

She's not club.

She's a fucking nurse.

Turn back.

He kept walking up those stairs to find the woman who'd given him the best orgasm he'd ever experienced. Opening one of the rooms he found it was a bare room apart from a single bed with no sheets on it.

Closing the door, he found Jessica's bedroom. It was a lilac bedroom with a darker purple bed. He liked the room instantly, and it shouted out Jessica's personality.

"What the fuck am I doing?" He didn't stop. She wasn't in the bedroom, and he saw the only door led into a walk-in closet.

Leaving the bedroom he found her lying in the bath tub. Bubbles were up around her neck, and she turned to look at him.

"I thought you were leaving?"

"I was going to leave."

"What changed?"

"I've got nowhere else to be. You're here, and we're going to spend some time together."

"You fucked me. Shouldn't you be leaving now? Don't you have some kind of moral code that says you can't fuck a girl twice?" she asked.

He placed their cups on the counter near the sink.

"I made you a coffee."

"You're not going to answer my question?"

"There's no need to answer it because I'm already sitting here." He took a seat on the toilet staring at her.

There were no signs of tears in her eyes or cascading down her face.

"I don't cry," she said.

He'd not even realized he'd spoken out loud.

"Why don't you cry?"

"I come from a family where tears are not really seen. We're a family of fighters. My dad's a lawyer. He's used to winning. Tears don't win court cases, good lawyers do. My brother, he's a doctor. He wouldn't be caught crying. My mom's a housewife, like those

Stepford moms you hear about. I don't cry."

Snake rubbed his hands together.

"Why did you walk away downstairs?"

"I'm not good with the whole morning after routine."

"It wasn't the morning after," he said, watching her.

Jessica blew out a breath. "I don't know how to do this. I've never had a boyfriend, not really. I've never lived with a man before."

"What?" He smiled. "I find that hard to believe."

"I've had plenty of sex. I've even had sex with same person. I've not wanted to have a boyfriend, and when I caught the one guy I was going steady with cheating on me, I haven't wanted to be with someone since." She shrugged. "I'm used to leaving afterward. I'm not used to sticking around and talking."

"Do you want a boyfriend?"

She shook her head. "No."

Snake didn't like that answer. This woman was going to reject him at every turn. She was in for one big fucking surprise. He wasn't going anywhere.

****

"Why are you still here?" she asked.

Jessica expected him to leave. She didn't anticipate him coming to find her. Staring over at him, she wanted to reach out and touch him, yet she couldn't bring herself to do it. What was it about him that he was breaking through all of her walls? She wasn't going to cry. Jessica couldn't remember the last time she cried. It was hard for her to admit the truth about not having a boyfriend.

"We're not finished."

"I don't want a boyfriend."

"I'm reading you loud and clear. You don't want

a boyfriend. I'm not going to force you to have one."

Wiping a hand down her face, she sat up to splash more water onto her face. "I don't know what you want from me."

"I don't want anything from you, Jess. I'm not going anywhere."

Frowning, she glanced over at him. He held out a towel, which she took. She didn't see the point in fighting him over a towel that she needed.

Drying her face, she returned her gaze to him. Her body still remembered and liked him. He was a big man, and he'd didn't have a clue that he was the first man to give her an orgasm with his mouth.

"I don't know what you want from me."

"How about we don't want anything from each other? I'm here because you want me here."

Thinking about Lydia, Jessica was hit by a wave of guilt. Her body was no longer held captive by arousal.

She's moved on to someone else.

"I want you here." She conceded that point. There was no point arguing there. She *did* want him. "I can't have you interfering with my work."

"Doctor Bastard doesn't get to go with you for coffee. He's out of the equation."

"You're making conditions of your own?"

"Yes. I want to fuck you without a condom. Get on the shot or the pill. I want to take your pussy bare."

"I'm not fucking you without a clean bill of health. I'm not an idiot. You've got a lot of pussy that could be infected at your disposal. I'm not going to risk my health for a quick fuck." She tilted her head to the side.

"Fine. We'll get tested tomorrow. Both of us, it's fair. When was the last time you had a man inside you?"

"About five minutes ago."

"Don't be cute. I mean for real."

She let out a sigh, glancing down at the bubbles over the surface of the water. He was really starting to get on her nerves, making her regret ever having sex with him.

"It has been over a year. Why?"

"I just wanted to know if there's anyone I had to kill."

"Kill?"

"Yeah, I don't like others touching what's mine."

Jessica frowned. "That makes absolutely no sense. You're with a biker group who shares women. The club whores?"

"So? I don't see you trying to be a club whore. You're not. You're mine, and like I said, I don't like sharing my things." He grabbed her cup of coffee, passing it to her. "I'm a little possessive over what's mine."

She took the cup from him, aware as he stroked her hair.

"Possessive?"

"Very."

"I've never had a possessive person in her life." The men she'd been with in the past were all happy to fuck and meet up later. She didn't know if she liked the risk of taking this to the next level with Snake.

"You're not getting rid of me. I'll let you break things to Lydia or I can."

"She's with someone else."

"Good," Snake asked.

"Are you jealous?" She took a sip of the hot coffee, wincing as it burnt her.

"No. I'm not jealous. It's easier for her to be with someone else."

"Well, at the moment I can't get in touch with

her."

Snake started to stroke the back of her neck. She found it difficult to breathe with his hands on her. He had such large hands, and the strength was a massive turn-on for her.

You're twenty-nine for crying out loud, not a teenager.

"Aren't you worried?"

"No. Lydia's one of these people who is known for going out on her own. I wouldn't worry about her. She always turns up eventually. With a story about how she met some guy." She bit her lip to stop herself from rambling. All she ever did was ramble these days.

"So there shouldn't be any backlash for me and you when she comes around."

"There shouldn't be, doesn't mean there won't be." The more she thought about Lydia, the sicker she got. "Will you stop touching me please?"

"Why?"

"I can't think with your hands on me."

He didn't stop. Snake wrapped her hair up exposing more of her neck. She loved the way he'd held her down, using her hair as leverage to fuck inside her.

Closing her eyes, she held onto the hot cup with a death grip.

"You're going to have to get used to me having my hands on you."

"I work a lot," she said, blurting the words out.

"You're going to have to take care of that as well."

"What do you mean?" He wrapped his fingers around her neck. Opening her eyes, she stared up at him. Snake lowered his lips to hers, pressing a single kiss to her mouth. "You either cut back your hours or I come and fuck you at work."

"I don't want a boyfriend."

"I'm not offering this to you as your boyfriend, Jess. I'm telling you this is how it's going to be."

"If you think I'm going to bow down to you in submission, you're wrong. It's not who I am."

He smiled. "I never took you for a submissive woman, Jess. I took you for a clever woman. I'm going to want to fuck you regularly."

"There better not be any other women."

"Why do you think I'm demanding you cut back your work? I won't have any other woman to fuck. The only one I want is you." He pressed kisses toward her ear, going to her pulse. She gasped as he sucked on her flesh.

"Stop. You're going to mark me."

"You're going to have my mark on your body. Doctor Bastard is going to know you belong to me."

"Stop talking about him."

"When are you going to realize I'm the one giving the orders?" He sealed his lips over hers, plunging his tongue deep into her mouth. She forgot about the cup of coffee in her hands, and she spilled some of the contents over herself.

Snake withdrew instantly, taking the cup from her. When he turned back to face her, he reached for the sponge and soap. Frowning, she watched as he lathered up the soap and motioned for her to stand.

"What are you doing?"

"I'm going to wash you."

"Erm, are you sure?"

"Stand up, Jessica."

He kept changing the way he said her name. One moment she was Jess, the next, Jessica. Everything about Snake confused her.

Standing up, she watched him. He stood outside

of the tub and started to wash her. He worked from her neck, going down. Snake covered his hand with soap, and he followed the sponge down, caressing over her body. She closed her eyes, trying to stop herself from gasping out when his fingers pinched her nipples.

"Keep your eyes open, Jess," he said.

Opening her eyes, she didn't stare at him but at the hand on her body.

"Spread those thighs." She opened her legs waiting for him to wash her with the sponge. Instead, his fingers slid through. They were no longer covered with soap. She felt the difference as he stroked her pussy.

Arousal began to build inside her. Before it even took effect, he moved on, leaving her wanting more.

"Lie down."

She sat in the bath feeling pissed that he was working her body to his advantage, not her own. The last thing she wanted to deal with was Snake's teasing.

He soaped her hair with shampoo, and when it came to conditioner, he took his time, washing through the strands. Not once did he catch a strand making her wince. Each second had her moaning in pleasure. He knew what to do to awaken a woman's desire. There was no denying that.

Snake urged her down into the water so he could rinse the conditioner from her hair. When it was over, he helped her out, dried her body, then helped her into bed, naked.

"I'm going to take a shower. I'll join you in a moment." She listened to the water running. Slowly, she closed her eyes, only closing them for a moment.

The last thing she remembered was Snake's humming in the shower.

Chapter Five

Five days later Snake wasn't in the best of moods. With Judi's premature son the club had banded together to prepare the clubhouse and Ripper's house. Lexie was staying close to the hospital as she only had a couple of months left on her pregnancy. Devil wasn't going to take any risks with her.

He didn't have his cell phone, and besides that first night with Jessica, he'd not seen her. They were finishing up the decorating of the nursery at Ripper's house. It was freezing cold, and they had to air out the rooms so there were no paint fumes remaining.

Snake was on assembly duty. He'd put together a cot and several pieces of furniture. What he didn't like was the fact he was also on shopping duty. Lexie had given Devil a list, which he'd given to Snake. Sitting outside the hospital, Snake tapped his fingers on the steering wheel. The little monster was doing fine. The club got regular updates from both Devil and Ripper.

Climbing out of the car, he walked on in. The receptionist on duty nodded at him. He gave her a smile before heading toward the room where Judi was. She was able to visit her son a couple of hours a day, but she was still being monitored. The C-section had been a huge success, but it was taking her some time to heal.

No one was with her, and she was staring down at his cell phone. Knocking on the door, he smiled at her as she looked up.

"Hey, Snake," she said.

"Hey, princess. I come bearing gifts." He held up the flowers, showing them to her.

"They're beautiful. You don't have to bring me gifts."

"Shall I take them away?" He pretended to walk

off.

"No, don't you dare. I want my flowers."

They were already in a vase, and he placed them beside the many bouquets she'd been sent.

"How are you holding up?" he asked, taking a seat.

"I'm nervous. I'm so nervous."

He took hold of her hand, squeezing her. "I know I was terrified that night. You could have just told us you were getting a little impatient."

She chuckled. "I never want to go through that again. Ripper's terrified. I don't think he'll be wanting another baby soon."

"I don't blame him. You've seen the little monster. He's adorable and cute. He'll be a handful."

"Ripper won't hold him," Judi said. "He's gone for some lunch. I sent him up, but whenever I'm with him, he won't hold our son. I've heard the nurses talking. He doesn't hold him when I can't." Tears filled her eyes. Moving onto the bed, Snake wrapped his arm around her.

There was nothing sexual to his holding Judi. She was the club princess. He didn't find her attractive. No, the woman plaguing him was a raven haired, blue eyed bitch. She wasn't a bitch, but he kind of liked calling her it. It was his own personal name for her.

"You've got to give him time. I imagine nearly losing you almost made him shit his pants. You're precious to us. Give him time."

"I've tried talking with Devil. He's not helping. He told me Ripper will hold our son when the time is right." She wiped the tears away. "I don't want him to not hold our son. We need to think of a name for him."

"Judi, you need to stop worrying. Everything will turn out okay."

"Will you talk with him?"

"I'll go and talk with him."

"Do you need your cell phone back?" she asked. "I left mine at home, and I always forget about it."

"Nah, kid, you have it until you get pictures for your own cell phone. He's at lunch?"

"Yes, please, talk to him, Snake. I'd appreciate it."

"Will do. Remember, you've got to rest." He pressed a kiss to her forehead, leaving the room. It didn't take him long to find Ripper. His brother was bent over a tray, eating. There was no life to him. He looked almost dead.

Grabbing a coffee, Snake took a seat at the table.

"I'm not interested in company."

"Good for you, I don't give a fuck."

Ripper looked up. "What are you doing here?"

"I've come to find Jessica to take her shopping." He pulled out the list for the little boy. "I've got to get this stuff."

He watched as Ripper read through the list. "You don't need to worry about that."

"What's going on with you?"

"Nothing."

"Nothing? You've got a son coming home soon. I heard he's been taken off the oxygen and is doing great, taking Mom's milk, and everything." Snake didn't want to think of Judi and her breast milk. The entire thought repelled him.

"What are you trying to get at?"

"We're all working hard to get that kid home safely, and you've not picked him up or held him."

Ripper stared at him for several moments without speaking. "It doesn't matter."

"No? Judi knows you've not held him."

"She doesn't."

"She does. Not only do you not hold him in front of her, she heard the nurses talking. You're breaking her heart in a time when she needs to get better." Snake took the list from him. "This is the stuff you and Judi should be doing. Your son came early. I get you're angry."

"You've got no idea how I'm feeling."

"Then talk to me because right now, you've got a woman who's scared about her son. He's fighting and proving himself even now that he's part of the Chaos Bleeds, yet his dad is eating alone." Snake sat back, staring at him.

"This is none of your business, Snake. Why don't you go back to stalking a fucking nurse who doesn't even fucking want you."

He was slowly breaking down Ripper's walls.

"What's the matter? Jealous? I don't have to be stuck at home with a woman and kid. I can fuck whoever I want."

"Stop it, Snake. You don't know what you're talking about."

"No? Then what is it? You don't want a kid anymore? Are you scared she's no longer going to love you but love someone else?"

He purposefully pushed Ripper until it finally came spilling out.

"He could have killed her, all right? How am I supposed to give a shit about it?" Ripper stopped talking as several people turned to look at him. He'd gotten up to start yelling. Snake stared up at him, pitying the man.

"Your son is a baby. What happened to him isn't his fault."

"I nearly lost her, Snake. Do you have any idea how hard that is to handle? I could have lost her, and I don't know if I've got what it takes to live with that."

"Come on. We'll get through this together. Judi could have died, but she didn't, and you need to remember that. She's alive and well." Snake stood, leaving behind his rancid coffee. "You're not eating the food. It's not even fit for dogs." Taking the lead, Snake made his way toward the neonatal unit. No one put up a fight as they moved toward the second room. After the baby was taken off oxygen and remained stable, he was moved up to the second room. Lexie was in the room. She wasn't holding the baby, just sitting watching him.

"What are you doing here?" Ripper asked. "I thought you were with Judi?"

"She didn't want me to be there. She asked me to come and check on your son." Lexie smiled up at Snake. "I'll leave you two alone."

"Look at him, Ripper." They were alone. The room only had one other baby, and there wasn't anyone else in the room.

Snake stood beside his brother, watching the little guy. He was fast asleep. His arms were up as he slept, completely innocent. There was nothing bad about him or evil. He'd not tried to kill Judi. A medical condition had nearly done that.

"He's beautiful," Ripper said.

Signaling to a nurse, he waited for her to come. "Don't you think it's time he got to see his dad?"

"Would you like to hold him?" the nurse asked.

Ripper removed his jacket, going to the sink, washing his hands. Snake took a seat as Ripper sat down. The nurse reached in and held the little guy in her arms. Snake watched as she placed the little bundle into Ripper's arms. "You need to support his head and body. There, I think he knows his father has him."

The nurse left the room, making sure the baby had a blanket around him before leaving.

"His eyes are open, Snake."

"He's saying hi."

Snake didn't leave, watching as Ripper held his hand against his son's. "He's holding my finger. Look at that, Snake."

Smiling, he glanced toward the window to see Lexie wheeling Judi into the room.

"You're holding him?"

"I am, baby. I'm afraid this time you're going to have to watch me hold him."

"I don't mind watching. You're holding him. I've not got a problem."

Snake stayed in his seat for the next hour. Only when he remembered the list in his pocket did he leave the room. He washed his hands, going to the reception desk.

"I don't suppose you could tell me where I could find Jessica?" He missed her and wanted to spend some time.

"She's gone to lunch." One of the nurses spoke up, looking frazzled as she went through several files in her arms.

Slapping his hand on the counter, he left, making his way up to lunch room.

****

Jessica stared down at the newspaper while she took a bite of her ham salad bagel. She didn't want to risk food poisoning from the chicken that looked like rock. Staring at the newspaper, she didn't read any of the words. It had been five days since she'd last seen or heard anything from Snake. She really shouldn't have been surprised. He wasn't the kind of man who could stick to anything, no matter what he said.

Like a fool, she'd gotten tested at the hospital, and she already had all of her paperwork back. She was on the pill and would be safe to have sex soon, not that anything was ever safe. The doctor she'd gone to had ranted about how only having no sex was safe sex. She'd gone a year without any sex. There was no way she was going to go another year. Even if Snake didn't want to fuck her, she'd find someone else.

She wasn't going to turn into one of those women who named their vibrators or bought cats, lots of cats. No, she was going to have lots of sex. It didn't help that she'd still not heard anything from Lydia. What she had found out was that she'd quit her job in town where she worked as a sales assistant in an accessory shop.

It was just like Lydia to move on without giving any consideration to anyone else around her.

"Hello there," Milford said, placing a tray opposite her.

The last five days they'd avoided each other. He'd moved onto another nurse, Bernie or something. She couldn't be sure. The work gossip wasn't something she was interested in.

"What do you want?" she asked, lowering her paper long enough to speak.

"You looked lonely here."

"I'm reading the paper. I don't need to have company for that."

"What happened to that man you were dating?" he asked.

"None of your business."

"Well, he's not here now, and so I'm getting my coffee."

"You're forcing coffee on me? Didn't you get a single thing I said to you?" she asked.

"I was listening, but I decided to take a step back and wait."

"Wait? For what?"

"For an opportunity like this." He placed a coffee in front of her. "I even went and bought you a coffee."

"Wow, you're very independent, ordering my coffee." She opened the cup to see it already had milk inside. "Have you spiked it?"

"No. I don't need to get my kicks out of using narcotics to get what I want."

She took a small sip. The coffee was rancid, but that wasn't anyone's fault. The coffee in the hospital was always rancid. It was how all the nurses and doctors stayed alert. "So why the sudden interest again? Am I next on your nurses list? I thought you'd move on to receptionists, fellow doctors, or maybe the rebel in you, patients."

"You really don't think well of me at all, do you?"

"I don't think about you at all, Milford."

He placed a hand over his heart as if he was hurt by her words. "You're a cruel woman."

Shaking her head, she took a sip. "I'm not going to sleep with you."

"You will."

"Ha," she said, forcing a laugh.

They both jumped as the spare chair at the table was turned. Snake lowered himself into it. "What did I tell you?" he asked.

The moment he talked, her pussy melted like ice in the sun. She'd missed him and hated herself for it.

"Sharing a coffee," Milford said.

She was really pleased he'd started talking. There was no way she'd form a coherent word. Snake was here, in the hospital. Judi hadn't been discharged yet.

"There's nothing going on here," she said.

"No?"

"No. I was minding my own business, and he

brought coffee."

Snake kept staring at her.

Believe me. Don't be a jackass.

He turned to look at Milford. "I'm going to warn you once and then I'll start to use my fists. Jessica is mine. She will always be mine. You're never going to get between her thighs because I'll always be there." He reached out, taking hold of Jessica's hand. "You're coming with me."

"Wait just one damned minute," she said, tugging her hand out.

"What? You want to stay here with Doctor Dick?"

"What? No, this isn't about that. God, five days, Snake. It has been five days since I've heard from you. Now you're pulling me around as if you own me."

"We're going shopping."

"No, we're not. I'm not going anywhere with you until you answer my question. Where have you been?" She folded her arms across her breasts. Her nipples were rock hard, pointing against her uniform. She didn't want him to witness her easy need for him.

"The nursery wasn't finished. There was still ten weeks to go for the baby to arrive. I've been helping decorate the club and his home. I've not had any time to get in touch. Judi has my phone with the pictures on. I can't take it off her. Not yet."

Now she felt like the worst person in the world. "I'm sorry."

"No need to be sorry. We all get jealous."

"I wasn't jealous."

"Just keep saying that." He took her hand, leading her toward the entrance and the parking lot.

"I can't just leave."

"I bet you're here on overtime. You work seven

days a week. Whenever do you take a break?" He made her sound so boring.

"I like my work."

"You're going to learn to like me a hell of a lot more than you like your work." He walked her toward a green car. It was nice, not very flashy but nice. "Get in."

She didn't argue, sliding inside. "Where are we going, or is this going to add to the list of kidnapping?"

"We're going baby shopping. I'm taking you to the mall. Are you okay with that?"

"Baby shopping?"

"Clothes, diapers, that thing they shove in their mouths."

"A pacifier?"

"Yes. We're going shopping for all of that."

"Why are we going shopping?"

"I got the short end of the deal." He pulled out of the parking lot. She noticed he paid careful attention to his driving. It was still icy, and snow was pushed in little mounds on the sides of the road. "Milford is a problem."

"He's a doctor, Snake. He's not a problem. Just persistent."

"I don't like him."

"I doubt a lot of men like him. I don't like him either. I'm not interested in the games he plays."

"The nurse games."

"Yeah. He likes to fuck as many nurses as he can. I hope they all gang up on him. It would be awesome to see." She chuckled, thinking about him being encircled by the women he'd fucked and dumped. "The same could happen to you."

"No. I only fuck women who know the score."

"Lydia didn't."

"She did know the score but decided to change the rules in her head. Crazy bitch." He made a whooping sound while also circling his fingers against his head.

"She's not crazy. She's just a little different."

"The bitch is crazy."

"The bitch is still my friend."

He was silent for a moment. "Have you heard from her?"

She glanced over at him and shook her head. "No, I've not heard from her. It sucks, but she's quit her job. She'll probably call me in a couple of weeks or months to let me know she's still alive."

"She's always been like this?"

"Yeah. Her dad is a businessman who travels. He used to leave her and her mother for months on end before he even called. Providing there was money, her mother didn't care. Lydia missed him though. She got the whole disappearing act from him. She's under some illusion that it makes people care about her a little more. It doesn't, but there you go." Jessica shrugged.

"And you're still friends with her?"

"I'm sitting in your car going to pick out baby items. I don't think I'm going to rate that high in the friends ranking." She tilted her head to the side to crack her neck. She did the same to the other side. "God, I'm tired."

"Don't worry about what she thinks, baby. Only worry about what you think about."

"That's how people end up lonely without any friends, Snake. You start caring about yourself and only yourself, no one is going to want to know you."

Chapter Six

Snake, with Jessica's help, carried through all the baby shit they'd bought on their trip. The conversation they'd had on the drive up to the mall was still ringing in his head. He wasn't lonely. He had a lot of brothers and women around him. The women didn't mean much to him, but his brothers did. He didn't always think about number one.

"Is this it?" she asked.

"No, we've got to make a stop at the clubhouse first." Snake closed the trunk of the car. "See you later, man," he said, shaking Spider's hands. He was the one house sitting for Ripper and Judi until they got out of the hospital.

"You're a reptile and he's an insect, why?"

"Baby, it's a long story to get involved into our names. Just know never to mess with me or if you like messing with me, never do shit that's going to involve me having to hurt you."

He turned the ignition over and pulled out of the street. This was the same street where Lexie and Devil lived, along with Vincent and his woman, Phoebe. Snake liked the street. It was a good one to raise a family away from the shit. When they'd first arrived in Piston County, the town had been separated into what looked like two parts, the good part and the bad part. The biggest problem was the bad part was most of the fucking town. Judi had been in the thick of that bad part, forced into prostitution at an age when she should have been giggling about boys behind her hand. Whenever he thought about what happened and what he saw, he wanted to kill the motherfucking pimp all over again.

"Have you killed people?"

"You're a nurse sworn to protect people. Don't

ask me a question you know you're not going to like the answer to."

"I've got a feeling I'm not going to like the answer to most things you do."

He glanced over at her, wanting to reach out and touch her, but knowing he couldn't do it, not yet. The roads were damned slippery, and most of the drive he'd taken slowly. He wouldn't even ride his bike in this weather. It was downright fucking dangerous, and he didn't have a death wish, especially not with Jessica in the car.

"Judi should be getting out in a couple of days."

"What about their kid?"

"They'll have to visit him. Most parents end up being discharged before the child. He's doing well though, strong. I asked one of the nurses about him. He's a fighter."

"He's part of Chaos Bleeds. We're all fighters in our own way." Not all of the members had come from a good family, with morals inbuilt into them like a second skin. Some of them came from shit homes, or foster homes, where they were used to fighting for their lives.

Snake, he was used to fighting for his life. Earning his keep on the streets and hurting anyone who stepped in his way. Devil had found him in the streets, too skinny to really fight, eating out of a damned trash bin. Running away from home had been better than taking another of his parents' beatings they liked to give him. Both of his parents liked to hit out at him, use him for sport to see how long he'd survive.

He hated them, and when he'd gotten fit and well, his parents had been his first real kill. Both of them had been shocked, pissing themselves.

Pulling up into the clubhouse, he pulled the keys out after parking up. He helped Jessica out of the car. She wasn't wearing any of those crazy assed shoes that women liked to wear. Her pumps went with the nurse's scrub outfit.

She followed him around to the back, grabbing a box as he did the same. Closing the trunk, he took the lead heading into the house.

Pussy was sitting at the bar nursing a beer.

"What's going on?" he asked. It was past six in the evening, but seeing Pussy look sad was a big deal. Out of all of the brothers, Pussy was known as the joker, rarely taking anything seriously.

"Not a lot. I was a fucking idiot, and I had to take Sasha to the hospital today for a fucking cast."

"Wait? What?" Snake asked.

"Yep. I'd moved the coffee table because my smokes had fallen underneath it. I moved it three inches. I forgot to tell her or put it back. She fell on the glass, cutting herself and breaking her damned arm." Pussy took another sip of his beer.

"I'm sorry, man," Snake said, slapping his friend on the back.

Sasha was Pussy's old lady, but she was also blind. It had happened when she lived at home with her stepfather. He'd slammed her against a wall, then thrown her downstairs in the effort to kill her. Sasha was blinded instead of dead. The doctors were at odds with each other over her condition. Some believe she'd get her eyesight back, while other remained convinced it would be permanent.

"Would you like me to take a look at the cast?" Jessica said, stepping forward.

"Nope. She's fine, just resting. Unless you can give me a cure for her fucking sight, I don't give a shit about anything else." There was a whine underneath Pussy. Snake glanced down to see Sasha's guide dog, resting his head on Pussy's lap. It was almost as if the dog knew Pussy was punishing himself. "It's okay, boy. I wouldn't have her any other way. You know that."

Pussy loved Sasha. He'd fought for her and been willing to walk away from the club to be with her. It looked like Pussy was having a hard time dealing with how delicate her condition was. Snake had watched as Pussy walked her around the clubhouse for days, getting her used to the layout of the place. No one moved shit unless Sasha was around. Even Dick didn't mess with the place.

"Come on. We'll take these up to their room."

He left Pussy to drink away his own guilt.

"Will he be okay?" she asked.

"Time will tell. I can't say for sure if any of us will ever really be okay with Sasha." Devil hadn't wanted her in the club, but it looked like even the Prez had taken a shine to her. Sasha was part of the club whether they liked it or not. Snake liked her. She was fun and hadn't let what the past did to her affect who she was.

They made their way upstairs.

"I know a little about Sasha's circumstances. When I'm next at work I could make a few calls. I'm not saying that it'll make a difference, but someone might have answers where others have failed."

He opened Ripper's door, leading the way in. "I'd appreciate that. The club would appreciate that. Sasha's an old lady, and she's part of the club."

Placing the box on the floor, he opened it up, and started to arrange stuff around the room. Jessica did the same. He didn't like the way she was making him feel right at that moment.

They worked without speaking, yet he was aware of her every move. The way she walked past him. The scent of strawberries surrounded her, driving him crazy.

When they were finished Ripper's room was more than ready for the baby.

"You all do this for each other?"

"When we were on the road, this wouldn't have happened. It's only because we're all settling down that we're getting shit like this done." Snake didn't have a problem with staying in the same place. Waking up on dirty mattresses beside a skank every morning had lost its appeal the moment he met Tiny and The Skulls. The club did show Chaos Bleeds another way of living. He wasn't going to be angry with Tiny or what had happened to separate them. They were living a whole new life now in Piston County.

"You were on the road a lot?"

"I was on the road my whole life. It never really stopped." Snake took a hand. "Come on. I want to show you to my room."

She didn't pull away.

The moment they touched it was like an electrical current ran through them bringing them both together.

He opened the door to his modest room.

"Wow, you're actually clean," she said, smiling.

Closing the door, he watched her look around his space. "I like clean open spaces." His parents had been drunks, and the place had been covered with filth where mold grew on the walls as if it was indeed the wallpaper.

The walls here were painted cream while the floor had a green carpet. His brothers wouldn't dare laugh at his space nor would the sluts that fucked the club.

"Snake, baby, would you like some company?" Amy asked, knocking on the door. He'd not been around the club whores in so long.

Jessica crossed her arms, staring at him. Her brow

was raised, waiting for him.

She knocked again. Everyone knew not to just barge into his space. He didn't like it.

"What's it going to be, Jessica?"

****

"What are you asking me?" Jessica wanted to open the door and claw the woman's eyes out. She didn't even know what the other woman looked like, but already, she didn't like her.

"Well, it has been five days and you were having lunch with Doctor Bastard. Do I call her in or am I already taken?"

"I got the clean bill of health. What did you get?"

He turned away, going to his drawer beside the bed. "I got a clean bill of health."

"You can't fuck me without a condom. I'm not protected yet."

"But we can in a few weeks." He gave her the sheet. "Amy knocking on the door is up to you."

"I go and you'll fuck her?"

"You go, we're over. It's the way I figured you'd play it. I'm not going to force you to be something you're not into."

"What do you mean by that?" she asked.

"I mean you're a nurse. The club is my whole life. I'm not going to change who I am. I'm a biker. I like having sex, and if you want us to be exclusive, I'll come to you every time. If you don't want that, I'll take you home."

"You're into exclusive sex? But Lydia—"

"Lydia doesn't know everything about me. She was a hole, Jessica. A woman to be used to fuck. You're not like her. Now, I'm either completely stupid and got the wrong vibe off you, or you're playing hard to get."

Jessica stared back at him. *Exclusive?*

"It's your choice. It will always be your choice," he said. "Can you hack this life?"

What she'd seen of the life hadn't been horrible. In fact, it had been an amazing support structure that was similar to a family.

"Snake?" Amy asked. Her voice already grated on Jessica's nerves.

Take a chance. What do you have to lose?

Her sanity. Her heart.

Snake wasn't just a scumbag who fucked women. Yes, he'd fucked Lydia, but he'd never actually promised her anything. Jessica was starting to see a whole new side to Snake, one she hadn't anticipated ever knowing.

Turning around, she opened the door staring at a beautiful blonde. She was slender with large tits. Jessica didn't like her. The malice in the woman's eyes was clear to see.

"You're not welcome here."

"I think that's Snake's decision."

Snake moved up behind her, gripping the back of Jessica's neck. "I'm doing whatever she says."

"He's mine now. You come here again offering your skank ass, I'll take you down. You even think to try and take him, I'll hurt you."

"What's a little nurse going to do to me?"

Jessica smiled. Before anyone got a chance to stop her, she shoved the other woman against the far wall, bringing her arm up against her throat. "You want to know what I can do to you? I can make sure you can't breathe. I know how to kill you and to make it look like a fucking suicide. Don't mess with me, bitch."

Releasing Amy, she took a step back. Snake stepped up behind her, wrapping an arm around her waist.

"You heard her." She was pulled back into the

room. The door closed, and he pressed her up against the door. "That was fucking hot, baby." His lips were on hers. Jessica pulled away, gasping for breath.

"I shouldn't have done that. I shouldn't have attacked her like that. It wasn't fair."

"Amy's a first class bitch, Jess. She'd have hurt you just to show she was the better person. You did right. In the club with the whores, you fight fire with fire."

"This isn't who I am."

"No? Then why did you do it?"

She licked her lips and his gaze wandered down to her lips.

"Tell me, Jessica. Why did you do it?"

"I didn't want her touching you. I don't like the thought of her hands on you."

"Then we've not got a problem. Any man touches you, do you think I'm going to let that happen?" She shook her head. "No, I won't. I'll fucking kill anyone who touches you. You're mine." He cupped her cheek. His fingers sank into her hair. When he was stopped by the band holding her hair up, he tugged it out. She winced at the sudden bite of pain that disappeared the moment his lips were on hers.

"I don't know what this is."

"Do you think anyone knows what this is?" he asked.

"No."

"Then let's not put anything to it."

They were exclusive, and she'd just acted like a possessive bitch claiming her man.

"Okay."

His lips were on hers in the next second. She wrapped her arms around his neck, holding on tightly to him. Gripping the hairs at the back of his neck, she tugged on the strands. Snake pulled away, slamming her hands above her head. She cried out from the strike of pain. With his other hand, he tore her scrubs open, destroying the shirt she wore. Within seconds he had her breasts out. His lips sucked on her nipples, awakening a need between her thighs.

"Are you wet?"

"Yes."

His hand moved down to slip into her pants. He pushed her panties aside, and she cried out. Roughly, he shoved two fingers inside her, plunging them in and out. The pads of his fingers were rough on her skin. She didn't fight him, trying to thrust down onto his fingers.

"I need your cock."

He went to his knees before her, tugging down her pants then her underwear. She bit her lip to try to contain her moans.

"Let me hear those sweet little sounds, Jessica."

Opening her lips, she cried out as his lips went to her pussy. There was nowhere else for her to go. He slid his tongue down to fuck into her pussy.

She tightened her fingers into his hair, panting as he fucked inside her.

He stood quickly, picking her up.

"Snake, what the hell are you doing?" She gasped as he flung her to the bed.

"We're doing this here." He tugged his shirt off, losing his pants in the process as well. "Get naked."

She flung off the remains of her shirt, and throwing the bra away. He was on her in the next second, opening her thighs. His hands were everywhere, holding her captive. Jessica didn't get a chance to touch or stroke him. Snake held her hands above her head at the same time he reached for his cock. He aligned the tip to her entrance and slammed home.

Crying out, she arched into his touch, trying to

get away, and trying to get him to go deeper.

"You're so fucking tight. I'm going to have to fuck this pussy until you can take me without it hurting." With his free hand, he caressed her cheek. "Does it burn?"

"Yes."

"Good. You'll remember me when you're walking around the hospital. Every time a man looks at you, you're going to know who you belong to."

She closed her eyes, wincing as he pressed a little deeper inside her. He was long and thick, so it was almost too painful to accept him within her. She wasn't going to push him away. When she finally softened, fucking Snake was the most amazing thing she'd ever done.

He kissed her lips, moving down to suck on her pulse. Snake sucked hard enough to leave a mark.

Jessica knew she'd have bruises around her wrists with the strength that he was holding her.

"You're so beautiful." He pushed himself up so that only his cock inside her and the hand holding her wrists touched her.

She couldn't hide as he stared down at her open body.

"What are you doing?" she asked.

"Looking at what's mine. That mouth with those thick red lips will look amazing sucking my cock, Jess. I want you to suck my cock."

She licked her lips, unable to resist teasing him just a little.

"Fucking bitch, you're doing that on purpose."

"Yes."

He pulled out of her only to slam inside. She cried out, arching up. The pleasure and pain combined together, shooting off nerve endings within her body that she didn't know existed. "You know what I can do to you, baby. Don't try to fight me."

Nodding, she stared up at him. He released her hands but only long enough to capture both with his hands. Snake held onto her wrists, pressing them to the bed.

He began to withdraw from her body.

"Watch me, Jess. Watch my cock."

Glancing down she saw his glistening cock, appear. He was naked, no condom.

"You've got to wear a condom. I don't want to get pregnant."

"Don't worry about it."

She opened her mouth to protest. He slammed inside, silencing her.

Snake didn't stop there. He pounded inside her, bringing her to the peak of orgasm but not letting her go over the edge. There was no point in begging or screaming. She couldn't voice her need as all she did was groan.

"Come over my cock, Jess."

He let go of her hand to play with her clit. Two strokes of his fingers was all it took to have her spiraling into orgasm.

She shouted his name as he rammed into her three times. He pulled out, covering her body, his seed spurting onto her stomach as his own release caught him.

They were both panting.

Jessica knew she should be pissed. He used sex to silence her, the width of his cock to keep her quiet, yet she couldn't be angry. Snake had pulled out. The risk was still there, but she was oddly touched.

Her life was getting way too complicated.

****

"This is interesting. Who's Jessica?" Master

asked.

Lydia lay on the floor, curled in a ball like he'd demanded. She shouldn't have gone away with him. With all of his riches and smooth talking, he'd tricked her. Tears leaked out of her eyes as she looked up at him. The brand on her thigh hurt. He'd done it two days ago when her cell phone had started ringing. She'd completely forgotten about the phone until then.

He hated being interrupted during a session. The cell phone had interrupted him.

"She's a friend."

"A friend?"

"Back in Piston County."

"A friend." He started looking through her phone.

They were alone in his room, which was a first. He liked to have men come in and take her. She'd heard him tell the men she wasn't anything special.

"Is this her?" he asked, showing her a picture of Jessica. It was one she'd taken at a picnic. Jessica wore a white summer dress that showcased her size sixteen curves. She knew Jessica's size because she'd been the one to buy the damned dress. Her raven hair looked so dark while her eyes caught attention with the startling blue color. He kicked out at Lydia asking the same question.

"Yes, it's her."

He nodded. "Good. She's pretty. Does she live in Piston County?"

She wanted to lie. If Master showed an interest it was only going to go badly for Jessica.

"Well, do you need another incentive to tell me the truth?"

She shook her head. "No, it's her, and she lives in Piston County."

"Well, well, well. It looks like that town gets

more enjoyable every day."

She was a horrible friend. The worst. She knew without a shadow of a doubt, she'd just brought pain to her friend.

Chapter Seven

Snake woke up to a head on his chest. He paused in stretching as it was the first time he'd ever woken up with a woman wrapped around him. Sure, he'd woken up next to women but rarely with them on him. Raven hair covered his chest, and he moved up the pillows so he was able to look down at her properly. She didn't wake. Her arm was over his waist and her leg over his.

He expected to be struck by panic at the sight of her. Nothing happened.

Stroking her hair away from her face, he saw she was still in deep sleep. Her mouth partly opened with her breath fanning over his chest hair.

The blanket covered her body, and last night came back to him. After he'd come all over her stomach, they had taken a nice long shower, washing each other. He'd ordered Chinese takeout and was able to grab the order before one of his brothers stole it. They were vultures when it came to food.

They ate in bed with the television playing some kind of horror movie. Jessica had chuckled through it, bursting out laughing at the blood scenes. She was the first woman he'd been with who laughed at gory scenes.

When he'd asked her about it she explained how unrealistic it all was. Being a nurse in the accident and emergency department opened her eyes to the horror movies. They had it all wrong.

He found her adorable. Sexy and adorable, a combination he'd never believed was going to be something that made him exclusive. Remembering last night, seeing her attack Amy and threaten her, had made him hard as fucking rock. His own parents hadn't fought for him, and yet Jessica had. She didn't want anyone else touching him or having him.

Snake hesitated in touching her naked shoulder. He couldn't believe he was lying in bed finding a naked shoulder sexy.

After they had eaten their Chinese, she'd pushed him to the bed, straddling his waist. She'd been the one to find the condoms he kept stashed. He'd forgotten the condom last night. The feel of her naked pussy was something he wanted to feel again.

Placing his hand on her shoulder, he stared down at where he touched her. What the fuck was happening to him? He was starting to sound like some kind of pussy.

"Morning," she said, snuggling closer to him.

He pulled away. "I didn't mean to wake you."

"It's okay. I should be getting up soon anyway. I've got to get to the hospital around eleven today."

"When does your shift end?"

"Eight tonight." She tightened her arm around him. "You're so warm."

"You're used to doing overtime right?"

"Yes. I can cut back my hours whenever it's needed."

"I want you to go back to your usual hours." He wanted the chance to spend more time with her.

"Why?" she asked, looking up at him. She covered her mouth.

"What the fuck are you doing?"

"Morning breath."

He cupped her face, slamming his lips down on hers. Plunging his tongue into her mouth, he stroked down her naked back to cup her ass. She moaned, rubbing against him.

"I don't give a fuck about morning breath."

"I get that."

Her hand started to stroke up and down his hip. His cock thickened at her closeness.

"You want me to reduce my hours?"

"Yes. I want to spend time with you."

She smiled, and he was hypnotized by her smile. Jessica was getting under his skin, and he didn't want to let her go, not ever. Wrapping his arm around her back, he locked their fingers together.

"Do you have a problem spending time with me?" he asked.

"No. I'll even take Lydia's wrath right now." Her gaze moved to where their hands were locked. "What's happening right now?"

"I don't know. I really don't know."

He took her hand, pressing a kiss to the tips of her fingers.

Jessica pulled her hand away. He watched as she slid her fingers down his chest. "I remember you saying something last night about sucking your cock?"

"I did."

She was nervous about what was happening between them. He saw it in her eyes, the doubt, the fear. She didn't know what was going on, and neither did he.

"Then I think it's time I give you something you want." She ran her hand down to cup his aching cock.

"I'll gladly have your lips wrapped around my cock."

She smiled. "And I'm more than happy to oblige." She started to stroke his cock, working her hand up and down his length.

Pre-cum already leaked out of the tip. He shoved the blanket off her so that he got a good look at her naked body. She was perfect. Snake never thought he'd love a woman with curves, yet he was addicted to the curves on Jessica. Her hips were bruised from where he held on tightly. Glancing at her wrists that were moving slowly over his cock, he saw they were bruised, too, each mark showing a sign of his possession over her.

Every man who saw her would know she belonged to another. Doctor Bastard better keep his fucking distance. Snake was more than happy with making people go to sleep.

Her lips lowered over his cock, and any thought process he had, vanished. Closing his eyes, he fisted his hand to try to stop himself from coming too quickly. She flicked along the tip, sliding down to take half of him into her mouth. Using her hands, she worked the rest of his cock so that he didn't notice he wasn't all in her mouth.

She worked him like an expert, cupping, nibbling, swallowing on his length. Jessica brought him to the peak and kept him at the precipice, leaving him begging to be pushed over. He wanted the orgasm that she could give.

Opening his eyes, he watched her head bobbing up and down over his shaft. Her hair covered the sight. Reaching out, he wrapped her raven locks around his fist. He saw his dick going into her mouth. The way her cheeks sucked in as she tried to take him as deep into her mouth as she could. The sight was almost his undoing. She looked so fucking beautiful.

He didn't want her to go to work unsatisfied.

Moving into the center of the bed, she released him long enough for him to move. Gripping her hips, he got her to straddle him so they were flush against each other with her over the top of him. Staring at her beautiful pussy, he opened the lips of her sex, sucking her swollen clit into his mouth. She moaned. The sound vibrated up the length of his cock. He released her pussy to work his fingers inside her pussy. Her cunt was soaking, and the more he teased her clit, the wetter she became.

When she took two fingers with ease, he started to push some of her cream back to the puckered hole of her anus.

She didn't tense up as he circled her ass, pressing slightly on it. He moved down to fuck into her pussy. Staring up, he pressed his finger to her ass, watching her tense up. Slapping her ass, he heard her yelp. "Relax," he said, biting the word out.

He watched her relax underneath his touch.

Working the slick tip of his finger into her ass, he went back to flicking her clit. She started to press back onto the finger in her ass, at the same time taking him deeper into her throat.

He felt her swallow around the tip before withdrawing. Sucking her clit, he filled her ass with a single digit. She came apart, her pelvis working on his mouth. He drank down her cum, finding his own release.

Jessica swallowed down his cum without complaint. When it was over, she collapsed over him so that her pussy was on his chest.

Pulling out of her ass, he lifted her up. He didn't give her a chance to protest as he carried her to the bathroom.

Neither of them spoke while he prepared the shower, waiting for it to warm up. There was no need for words as they both stood in the shower. He washed her body while she washed him. She'd washed him twice now, and he didn't like how much he was enjoying it.

When the shower was finished, he dried her down.

"I'm going to drop you off at work, and I'll pick you up."

"Okay, I'll, erm, I'll cut my hours down so they're normal. No overtime."

"What about being called in? That one night on

our date, you were called in."

"All nurses are on call. I can put my name off the list if you'd like. I've only been called in a handful of times since in the last couple of years."

"Take your name off the list. I don't want you being called away in the middle of the night."

"Sure. I'll, erm, I'll do that." She bent down to pull on her pants.

"Your underwear?"

"They're dirty. I don't wear the same underwear."

Going to his drawer, he pulled out a pair of his briefs. "Wear these. They'll be big, but I won't have to think about all the men staring at your ass."

"You're, erm, you're very possessive. I wouldn't have thought that about you."

"Neither would I."

"This is new to you then?"

"Very new," he said.

He looked through his wardrobe and handed her a shirt. "Wear this."

She took the shirt without argument. For several seconds they looked at each other, neither saying anything, and yet, their gazes saying a lot.

Snake was in trouble. He knew that more than anything. When it came to Jessica, he was in trouble.

****

Jessica signed off her patients listening as Milford organized the discharge papers for Judi.

"I doubt this will get rid of the biker group, but at least she's well," he said to a giggling Bernie.

Rolling her eyes, she finished looking through the latest chart. She was pleased Judi was doing well. Her little boy was as well, and it looked like he could be out by the middle of February. He was a strong little guy.

Milford stood directly behind her.

"Are we good to get coffee?" he asked.

"Nope."

She ticked the necessary boxes and handed the chart back to the reception desk. The woman on the desk looked at her with pity. Without saying anything more she left the main desk and started back to the emergency room. It was a slow day with barely any visitors. Several of the Chaos Bleeds crew were still there waiting. She'd not seen Snake since he'd dropped her off. She didn't know what to make of her current situation with Snake. One moment she hated him, then she wanted to have sex with him, then she wanted to laugh and joke with him.

She'd never been in love with anyone, and yet, she was sure what she was starting to feel was love. Going to the coffee machine, she paid the money in, clicking for a black coffee.

"You're going to have a coffee out of the machine instead of sitting with me?" Milford said. He still hadn't disappeared.

"This machine isn't trying to get into my pants every chance it gets." She turned around to look at him. "Let it go. I'm with someone."

"The biker? You can do so much better than that."

"I own a bike. I like bikes, and I like men who ride bikes. Don't start to think you know me."

This guy reminded her a little of her father, which was just eww. She wouldn't screw anyone like her father. Men like him always looked down their noses at other people.

"You ride a bike?" he asked.

"Yeah, I ride a bike, and I fuck men who are unsuitable. You're not even in the same league as me, Milford. Back off, as otherwise Snake's going to have an issue."

"I already have an issue," Snake said. He appeared behind Milford, grabbing the doctor around the neck, and pressing him against the wall. Jessica threw her full coffee into the trash rushing to Snake.

"Nothing was happening, Snake. He's not worth getting into trouble over." She tugged on his arm, trying to make him let go. Nothing was happening. He wouldn't budge. "Snake, please, let him go."

"No, I'm not going to get into trouble," Snake said. He shoved Milford into the wall one final time.

"You will. I'm telling the cops. This is assault."

"Wrong answer." Snake gripped him tightly around the neck again, practically throwing him about like a rag doll. "Let's get one thing straight, you piece of shit. You tell on me or you look at Jessica again, I'll come after you. There are enough women in this hospital who'd be happy to get rid of your ass. You're fucking scum, using your place to lure women into bed. I hear you doing it again I'll take this further."

"You can't kill me."

"No? Actually, I can, but you're right. It would be much more rewarding watching you squirm on the stand. Your career and reputation in tatters." Snake slammed his fist into Milford's gut. "Let's go, Jess."

She didn't argue, taking his hand.

With her changing her hours, she'd texted him to let him know she'd be finished by one o'clock as today was her day off.

Several of the nurses were happy with her reducing her hours as it meant they could book the overtime in. If she'd known she was stopping women and men from earning more money, she'd have stopped ages ago.

She didn't need the money as she came from wealth. Her father, no matter how much he was pissed off with her over moving to Piston County, wouldn't disinherit her. Her mother was proud, and Jessica learned long ago to make sure her mother was happy, and her father wouldn't say anything against her.

"You didn't have to do that," Jessica said, following him out to the parking lot.

"He was only going to get worse. Men like Milford don't understand the word no. I fucking hate men like that." Snake helped her into the passenger side of the car.

"Judi and Ripper are going home today."

"They're going to be at the club. We're all having a celebration."

"What are you celebrating?" Jessica asked.

"Right now we're celebrating the fact Judi is alive and well. When the little monster comes home, we'll celebrate him." She watched as another car pulled into the parking lot. "Devil's here now. Give me a moment."

He closed the door walking toward the other member. Devil wore a leather jacket showing the club he ruled. She'd seen him up close, and on the front there was a tag with the name "PRESIDENT". It was all in capital letters making no mistake who he was.

The woman, Lexie, climbed out of the car. She was swollen pregnant, but the stress of Judi hadn't caused any problems for her. It wasn't her first child but her fourth.

Snake and Devil shook hands before he started making his way back to the car.

"What was that all about?"

"I was telling him about Milford. He's going to look into the fucker."

"He's just a sleazy doctor, Snake. I think you're worrying about him a little unnecessarily."

"It's either look into him to keep him away or I'm going to do something I regret."

"I can't believe you can talk about killing him so easily."

He gripped the back of her neck, slamming his lips down on hers.

"I can talk about it easily, because it's the truth. I don't like the thought of anyone having their hands on you." He stroked her neck then pulled away.

"So, this party tonight?"

"You're coming."

"Wait, what?" She wanted to stay in with a good book or at least a good movie.

"Devil wants to meet the girl that scared Amy."

She frowned, turning to look at him. "No one saw that but us."

"Amy's got a big mouth. She's told all the women to steer clear of me. It looks like you got your message across."

She groaned, dropping her head into her hands. "This is bad."

"Why's it bad?"

"I've never been to a club party. I don't even like drinking, Snake. God, they're all going to laugh at me, and worse, they're going to laugh at Amy."

"No, they're not. We're going to your house so that I can get you prepared tonight."

"This is all wrong."

"We're exclusive," he said.

"What does that have to do with it?"

"We date each other. You've scared away other women. You're coming to this party because it's important to me."

She stared across the car at him as he pulled out of the parking lot. "Are we like boyfriend and girlfriend now?" she asked.

"We're certainly something. Do you want to put a label on it?"

"I don't know what I want to do."

"Well, I figured we could stop off at the diner, eat some burgers, and go to your place."

She nodded. "It sounds good."

Twenty minutes later, he pulled into the parking lot around the back of the diner.

"I'll be happy when spring shows itself," she said, wrapping her jacket around her. Snake pulled her close, wrapping his arms around her body. His warmth seeped through her clothes.

"I can warm you up."

She melted against him, not wanting to let go. They walked into the diner, finding a seat in the back. One of the waitresses took their order within seconds of them being seated.

"Mia, Curse's old lady, made sure we got served."

"I remember hearing something about you not being all that popular here."

"It's settling down a little. I think proving we're not thugs is helping," he said.

"They're keeping a close eye on that strip club you're organizing."

"The strip club?"

"Yep, I've heard a lot about it. The wives in town want it shut down while the husbands want it open. Will this be one of those clubs where the girls add a little extra in the back rooms?" she asked, smiling.

"I really can't say."

She shrugged. "It doesn't matter. I'll never be visiting."

"Why not?"

"Always busy. I'm not in need of seeing a woman's tits on display, Snake. I've got a set of my own. I want to watch them swing, I'll dance in front of a mirror."

One of his brows rose as he stared at her.

"I may get you to show me some of those moves."

She chuckled. "You're a horn dog, anyone tell you that?"

"You know they do."

The smile left her face as she thought about Lydia.

"Have you heard from her?" he asked.

"Who?"

"You know who." He gave her a pointed look.

"No. I've not heard from Lydia."

"Do you want me to look into her?"

Jessica shook her head. "There's no point. Lydia will appear when she wants to. I've come to see over the years that I've been the stable one. Lydia, not so much."

Their burgers came, which stopped anymore talk. She didn't want to talk about Lydia. The guilt had started to fade, and even thinking about her now, she didn't feel guilt for being with Snake.

She was a horrible friend.

Chapter Eight

"You know I was supposed to be helping you pick out an outfit, not sitting here waiting." Snake shouted the words for Jessica to hear upstairs. They had a great time eating their burgers, laughing and joking. The moment they got indoors, Jessica disappeared upstairs to get ready. It had been thirty minutes, and he'd hoped to get her naked.

The party wasn't for another couple of hours.

Glancing across the room, he checked out the time to see they had another couple of hours to spare. They could turn up at any time. Devil had already called him to let him know Judi and Ripper were at the club.

The visiting times were not great for visiting their baby. The good news was the fact the baby was doing great. He should be home within a matter of weeks.

"Okay, I want you to close your eyes and not peek."

"How can I peek?"

"Just do it."

Closing his eyes, he called out to her that they were.

He heard movement and was tempted to peek. Remembering the way she attacked Amy last night stopped him. He didn't want her hurting his balls.

"Right, you can look," she said.

Opening his eyes, his cock went rock hard at the sight. He'd never been so aroused so quickly. She wore a very tight red dress that molded to her curves like a second skin. Her hair was curled, and the length cascaded around her in luscious waves. The makeup she wore was minimal only highlighting the plump red of her lips and her rosy cheeks. The black mascara she wore emphasized her blue eyes. The whole package was wow.

He was going to be the envy of every single guy at the club.

"I don't wear short skirts or any revealing stuff. This is all I have. I wore it for dinner with the family a year ago. I've not worn it since."

His mouth was dry as she turned. The back dipped down, showing a little flesh. There wasn't enough to show off the bra she was wearing. Was she even wearing panties?

"Do I look okay?" she asked. Her hands went to her hips, and then her fingers locked together in front of her.

"You're beautiful." He stood up and closed the distance between them. Wrapping his hands around her body, he pulled her closer. She was so fucking sexy. Sexy and hot and he couldn't keep his hands off her. "Damn, baby, I don't want to take you to the party." He slid his hand down to her ass. There wasn't even a sign of a thong. He pushed his hand up the inside of the dress.

"Snake!"

She was bare and wet to the touch.

"Will you stop that?" Jessica pushed him away. He licked the cream off his fingers.

"You're so fucking beautiful."

"And you keep saying that. How do I look? Will I fit in?"

"You're going to stick out, baby. Every man will want you tonight. The sweet-butts are going to hate your ass." He tugged her close, pressing his nose against her neck. Breathing her in, he rubbed his cock against her stomach. "Do you feel what you do to me?"

She moaned, and he gripped her ass. "We're going to that party."

"We are."

If he could get his dick inside her, she'd stop

talking about the party.

"Snake?"

"Yeah?"

"Party."

"Fine, fine," he said, withdrawing his hands. "We better go now otherwise I'm going to bend you over the couch, table, or bed, and fuck you."

"I like the sound of that, but we can do that after this party."

She held her hand up stopping him from taking the moment further.

He counted to ten inside his head, trying not to look at Jessica.

Once they were in the car, he found himself glancing toward her. He couldn't help it.

By the time he parked the car at the clubhouse parking lot, he was still hard as rock.

"Imagine Lydia," she said.

"What?"

"With your little problem, imagine Lydia. She scared you, freaked you out a little. It should help." She smiled over at him.

"You're doing this to torture me."

"No. I'm doing this to fit into your world, Snake. I've accepted there's something between us. I can't explain it, and to be honest it scares me. I've never been with anyone like you before. You can't deny something is going on."

"I can't." He agreed with her. There wasn't a point in lying about the truth.

"I'm going to try to fit in with your world." She opened the door, and Snake took a breath. He had a feeling she was going to fit into his world a little too well.

As Snake walked her toward the clubhouse door,

Dick was standing at the door.

"Wow, fuck me, man."

"Shut up, Dick."

"You're the nurse who helped Judi?" Dick asked. Snake watched him throw the cigarette to the ground, stomping it out.

"Yes, that's me."

Dick held his hand out. "I appreciate everything you did for Judi and the club."

She took his hand. "Thank you."

The respect Dick had for Jessica was clear to see. Snake frowned at Dick. The other man wasn't known for being nice. He'd earned his name by being a dick to almost anyone.

They entered the clubhouse. Lexie was arguing with Devil.

"I've told you to sit your ass down on a seat. You're pregnant, and I want you to rest."

"Nothing is wrong with me, Devil."

"Do you want me to take you over my knee? I fucking will in front of the whole club."

"You dare and I swear you won't have any sex for a year."

Both of them stared at each other, glaring.

"Lex, Devil's right. You need to sit down," Judi said, walking downstairs. She looked so tiny, vulnerable. Ripper held onto her shoulders, staying close to her. He didn't like seeing Judi like this. "We've already had one scare."

"You should be upstairs, resting."

"I know you're throwing a party. I'd rather get stuck in here."

"This is going to be a lame assed party," Spider said, walking around the bar.

Judi shook her head. "It's not going to be a lame

assed party. It's going to be a damned good one. I won't have anyone telling me that a party of mine is lame." She walked over to the music player, and selected a song. "Ha, this will do."

Snake pulled Jessica against his side. "How is she doing?"

"She'll be fine. Providing she takes rest, and everyone keeps up her spirits. Everything should be fine now. The biggest problem is the baby. He could take a turn at a moment's notice. It's why he's staying in the hospital so they can keep an eye on him."

"Jessica?" Lexie said.

They all turned toward them. Snake saw the interest in the single men's eyes. Gripping the back of her neck, he sent a glare out to all of them. This woman was his. None of them had a chance.

"I brought you a nurse, Devil," Snake said.

"Finally a woman of sense." Devil walked up. "Tell my very sexy, but very stubborn, wife that she must rest."

Jessica smiled. "Lexie, I'm afraid I'm going to have to agree with your husband. You really need to rest. You've had quite a scare with Judi. It wouldn't be right for me to say otherwise. Rest, you're heavily pregnant and really need to take care of yourself and the baby."

Devil cheered while Lexie huffed.

"Please don't hate me," Jessica said.

"You're the nurse. You know what you're talking about whereas this big lug doesn't. He's only happy that you agree with him. I heard what you did to Amy."

He watched as Jessica glanced down. "I'm sorry—"

"It was about time someone put her in her place. She was getting a little too full of herself." Lexie patted her on the arm. "Some of the sweet-butts really think they can just fuck our men and we'll not do anything. I'm pleased you showed them it wasn't the case."

"And it made me hard as rock," Snake said.

"Ew, too much information. Thanks for the visual." Lexie covered her eyes and shook her head. "Have fun at the party."

Snake tugged her back against him. "You're going to have a lot of fun."

"I really am sorry about that girl."

"Don't say anything and spoil my fantasy. The only thing missing was lubricant or mud. I don't know which one would have been more appealing."

"Has anyone told you that you can be a real horn dog?"

"Only you." He wrapped his arms across her rounded stomach. "And now I'm only horny for you."

Tilting her head back, he sealed his lips over hers. For the first time since they got together in front of others, Jessica melted against him. She did so in private but never in front of people. Even in the diner earlier, she hadn't relaxed. He wanted her to relax around him so that it was natural to her.

"What are you doing to me?" she asked, whispering the words against his lips.

"I could ask you the same thing." He was changing, and it was all down to this one woman in his arms.

****

Later that night the party did finally pick up. Judi and Ripper were on the dance floor. The happy couple had already been congratulated and was now dancing close together. Jessica leaned against one of the walls, sipping from a can of soda watching Ripper and Judi dance. Snake had left to have a smoke with a couple of the men. She saw there were a lot of men, and a lot of women from town. Some of the women were the club whores that Snake told her about while others were just women who wanted sex.

"Hi, you're Jessica right? I'm June." A slender woman stood in front of her offering a hand.

"Hello," Jessica said, without taking the offered hand.

"I'm one of the club whores," she said.

Raising a brow, she stared at the other woman wondering if she was stupid or silly.

"I heard what you did to Amy. I wanted to come and be honest with you."

Standing up, Jessica stared at the pretty woman. She had brown hair, with pretty green eyes.

"Well, have you come to stick up for your kind?" Jessica hated being a bitch, but Snake did warn her that the only way to survive with these women was to be harsh. It was what they knew.

"No. I fuck the men who aren't available. I wouldn't dream of being with the men who are. Believe it or not, I actually have some morals."

"You've never fucked Snake?"

"I didn't say I'd never fucked him. I've never fucked Devil or Ripper. They were taken even before I came around. Snake, he wasn't seeing anyone when I arrived."

"Why do you sleep with lots of men?" Jessica asked, no longer hating the woman. She couldn't exactly bitch at her for being honest and human. Snake was a good looking man.

"I like it. You like being a nurse, I like fucking men. I'm not ready to settle down nor do I want to. I have an itch that needs to be scratched just like every other woman."

Jessica smiled. "Stay away from Snake and we'll

call ourselves even."

"You're not going to chase me down with the intent of killing me?"

"No. Do as I ask and I'll let you live." Jessica laughed. "I'm only kidding. I'm a terrible actress."

"Not at all. I'm glad I came over here. I'm going to look so tough to the rest of the women. They're afraid."

"Why?" Jessica asked, taking a sip and looking around the room.

"They'd fuck Snake in a heartbeat, and it wouldn't have anything to do with you."

"He's well endowed," Jessica said, smiling. She liked the size of his cock. It sometimes made up for his personality.

"I've got a feeling I'm going to like you."

"Likewise."

They both started to dance to a beat.

"Come on, there's more fun to be had out there on the dance floor. Most of the single men are looking at your smoking body. I can have the leftovers that Snake doesn't kill." June took her hand, leading her toward the main throng of people. Judi and Ripper were in their own little secluded corner away from the heavy beat of the music.

"Let's get this party started," June said.

The music was turned up, and the beat bounced off the walls. June took Jessica's soda from her. "Come on, let's dance."

June wrapped her arms around her and they danced close. Dick pulled June against him and he started to rub his dick against her ass. Ignoring the men, common sense, and just focusing on fun, Jessica threw her hands in the air and started to sway her hips to the beat. Men came up and danced with her. When they got a little too close, she pushed them away. Closing her eyes, she basked in the fun. June came back and disappeared. Jessica missed Snake and wanted him close.

Someone wrapped their arm around her waist, thrusting his cock against her ass.

Before she could stop whoever was holding her, she heard Snake's voice.

"Dime, get the fuck off my woman."

"This is your woman?"

Opening her eyes, she stared up into the dark depths of her man. He looked so jealous that it gave her a thrill to see. "This is my woman, and you're a second away from being unable to father children, Dime."

The man behind her let her go. Jessica threw herself into Snake's arms. "I wondered how long you were going to be."

"You missed me? It didn't look like it from where I was standing."

"I was about to throw him off me." She pressed her lips to his, moaning as he plunged his tongue into her mouth. His hands gripped her ass tightly, thrusting his pelvis against hers. "You got there before I was allowed that pleasure. There's only one man I want."

"You've got him."

The room fell away as Snake showed her exactly who she belonged to. She didn't want to be in anyone else's arms nor in his bed. Snake was the man for her, and that was what terrified her.

Judi and Ripper were the first to leave the party, followed by Devil and Lexie.

"Come on, I've got a cock with your name on it."

"Wow, you're so romantic," she said, rolling her eyes.

He took her up to his room. She hadn't been drinking, but she wanted to be with him. The clubhouse was fast becoming her home. Snake closed the door, turning to her quickly. Before she knew what was happening he pushed her dress up, taking her back toward the bed.

"I can't wait any longer."

"Please, Snake, I need you inside me."

He dropped her to the bed. Going to her elbows, she watched as he unbuckled his belt, dropping his jeans far enough. His cock sprang free. He was already long and hard. She opened her thighs, reaching down to stroke her clit.

"Do you want my dick, baby?"

"You know I do. I need you." She slid a finger inside, crying out at the pleasure.

Snake shoved her hand away, replacing her finger with the tip of his cock. There was no time for condoms. Even Jessica couldn't bring herself to stop him.

He slammed to the hilt inside her. The thick length of his dick scraped down her walls, and she whimpered as he plowed inside her. He didn't stop until he was balls deep within her.

"Fuck, baby. You're always so tight and so wet. This is my addiction. This is what I want. I'm addicted to you, Jess. So fucking addicted."

He leaned down, biting onto her shoulder. They were not touching enough skin. Snake tore at her dress. The sound of fabric tearing filled the room.

"I'll get you a new dress, baby." His lips sucked on her nipple, biting down as he also thrust inside. She thrust up to meet his cock. Jessica tugged up his shirt, throwing it out of the way. Scoring her nails down his back, she panted for breath at the intense pleasure of his cock thrusting inside her.

"Fuck, yes. Put your mark on me, baby. Put your fucking hands on me. Touch me. I want it." He groaned, pounding inside her. The strength of his thrusts made the headboard hit the wall, matching the pounding of his hips. He was stroking along her G-spot, his balls slapping her ass.

She scratched his back, crying out as he hit her cervix. The pleasure was so intense that it was almost pain.

"You're all mine. I'm never going to let you go, never ever. You're mine now."

"Yes," she said, moaning as he sucked one nipple then the other into his mouth. She was so close to orgasm

He pounded inside her, over and over. She reached down, touching her clit. With each thrust of his hips, he smashed her hand against her clit adding an element of pain.

Jessica couldn't hold off any longer. She screamed out as her orgasm struck her hard. Snake didn't stop. He kept fucking her hard.

When he did come, he threw his head back crying out his release. The sound echoed off the wall, giving her goosebumps. He slumped down over her.

"Fucking hell, baby, you're going to send me to an early grave with that sweet pussy of yours."

She chuckled. "You weren't too bad yourself."

They finished removing their clothes. Jessica felt his seed sliding out of her pussy, but for some strange reason, she didn't seem to mind.

The party was still going on in full swing downstairs.

"I saw you talking with June."

"Yeah, I did."

"What did you think of her?" he asked.

"I know that you fucked her. I also know that June doesn't fuck any of the men who are taken. Don't worry. I'm not going to cut your balls off. I'm not that horrible a person." She chuckled. "How did you know I was talking with June? I thought you went out for a smoke."

"I did. I came back in, saw you with June and ran. I didn't want to be caught up in the crossfire with you two."

"You're a coward."

"Only when it comes to you. Do you know how to fire a gun?" he asked.

Shaking her head, she chuckled. "No gun, but I do know how to fire a weapon."

"See, you're terrifying me already."

Jessica slapped him. "I like June, and, erm, I kind of like you." She admitted the truth to him.

"You like me?"

"Just a little and only kind of like you." She stared down at his chest, wondering what the hell was making her say these things.

"Well, I kind of like you, too. I like you a lot actually. You're the first woman I've ever taken the time to talk to."

"Really?"

"Yep, I don't believe in talking to a woman about anything. I like sex. With you, it's different. I get the feeling it's always going to be different with you."

"Snake?"

"Yeah, baby?"

"Don't cheat on me okay? I don't want to be one of those women who find their man in bed with another woman. You want to end this, do it to my face with words. I can't stand the thought of being hurt like that."

"I'm not going to hurt you. I promise." He leaned down, pressing a kiss to her lips. It was tender, sweet, and Jessica knew in that moment she was falling in love with him.

****

"Ripper and Judi are holding up well," Lexie said.

Devil walked into the bedroom, drying his hair with a towel. His woman wore a silk negligee that was rather tight across her stomach. Some men wouldn't like her abundant curves, but to him, she was the most beautiful woman in the world. She'd gotten even more beautiful since she'd given him children and also taken Simon on as her own.

"They've been through a lot already."

"I called Eva. Tabitha's doing much better, and everything is settled. Tiny's handed over the gavel to Lash."

"I didn't see that one coming so quickly." Devil threw the towel into the laundry basket, then the one wrapped around his waist. He padded over to the bed barefoot. Lexie was struggling to lie down. "Come on, baby, let me help you."

"You must think I'm a beached whale."

"Not at all. You're the most beautiful woman in the world." He voiced his earlier thoughts while also easing her into bed. "This to me is beautiful." He cupped her stomach, pressing a kiss to the rounded bump.

"You're a charmer."

"I'm your man." He climbed over her, settling behind her back completely naked. Resting his hand on her stomach, he kissed her exposed shoulder. "Ripper and Judi have the whole club at their back."

"I just worry. A premature baby is going to be hard work. There's medicines, and we've got to take precautions."

"The men love her like their own. They're going to take care of her, and no one will care about the work." He caressed Lexie's stomach, wishing she'd calm down.

Devil didn't like her getting stressed. It wasn't good for her or the baby.

"I know I shouldn't worry."

"You can worry but worry about the right things."

"Oh, yeah, and what are the right things?"

He caressed up her body to cup her jaw. "The right things are to make sure your man is taken care of, our kids, and the club. We're in this together. I won't let anything happen to Judi or Ripper or the baby."

"You'd have made the same choice with me though."

"I would. You come first, always. I love the kids, but I don't love them the way I love you. They're my flesh and blood, you, you're my life, Lexie. You're something I can't give up." Pressing his lips to hers, he moaned as she opened up to him. They'd been together nearly five years, maybe longer, and he still couldn't get enough of her. She was his whole world.

Chapter Nine

Four weeks later Ripper and Judi's baby, whom they'd named Paul, was allowed to come home. The whole club arrived at the hospital. There hadn't been many of the brothers who had the stomach to see Paul in the neonatal unit. Snake stood behind Jessica, his woman. The past four weeks had been out of this world. When neither of them was working, they were together. They slept at the club or at her place. He'd taken her to the movies, to dinner, and they'd stayed at the clubhouse.

She still hadn't heard from Lydia, which he didn't mind. The woman was crazy, and while Lydia was away, it meant he got his woman all alone without worrying about a friend's interference.

What he was happy about was Doctor Bastard's withdrawal. The man had taken his threat seriously, and one night after Jessica fell asleep, Snake had paid the good doctor a visit at his own home. He made sure Milford knew his place and that Snake could kill him whenever he wanted without a thought.

"Look at them, Snake," she said, touching his hand with her own.

"They look beautiful together." He pressed a kiss to her head. For the past four weeks Judi had been a shell of her former self. Leaving the baby every day had hit the young couple hard. Fortunately, nothing had gone wrong, and Paul was as strong as ever. Glancing toward Devil, he saw Lexie and the kids were also in tow. Lexie had her hand on her abdomen. She should be dropping any day now. Devil had already put them on water breaking warning.

When Elizabeth was a couple of weeks from being born, Devil made all of the club aware of what could happen at a moment's notice. Snake hadn't liked watching Lexie's feet in case of a puddle, but he'd done it for his Prez. Now, he understood why. He understood more than most.

"You better show that little darling off," Phoebe said, rushing forward. Judi held Paul in her arms while Ripper held the car seat they needed to put him in. Paul was still small, but with time, he'd fill out. "He's so cute. I can already see he's going to have all the girls chasing after him." Phoebe was Vincent's wife.

"I think someone's feeling broody."

"You think Phoebe wants more kids."

"Yep, look at Vincent. He looks scared to death." Jessica chuckled.

"Do you want kids?" he asked. He'd not given kids a thought. Jessica was opening his world up making him want things he'd not even realized he wanted.

"Someday I guess. I'd not really given it much thought. You're supposed to want them, right?"

"A lot of people seem to think it's the way forward."

Jessica shrugged. "I've never had the yearning to have a family of my own. There's not been a man out there who has awakened that yearning."

He didn't take offence. For the both of them this was entirely new territory. For the last five weeks the only pussy he'd had was hers. He was used to being bored now, but alas, that hadn't happened yet. Snake kept expecting it, too, but it hadn't happened.

"I've got a problem," Jessica said, turning toward him.

"What's the problem?"

She ran fingers through her hair, twitching a little as she looked left and right. "Erm, Lydia hasn't called, but my dad and brother have."

"Your dad and brother?"

"Yeah, they're stopping by Piston County tomorrow and they want to have dinner."

"Is this great or not?" he asked.

"I don't know. I was wondering if you'd like to come and meet them?"

He paused. "You want me to meet your parents?"

"I want you to meet my parents and my brother, if you don't mind." She bit her lip.

"Why?"

"Well, they're always worried about me. They don't think it's good for me to be alone, and when they find out that Lydia has done another disappearing act, they'll be pissed."

"What's Lydia got to do with it?"

"We've been friends along time. My parents preferred me moving to Piston County so long as I had a friend here."

"They don't know about her regular disappearing acts?"

"I'm a twenty-nine-year-old woman. I don't tell them everything."

He let out a sigh. "I'm there to show you're protected?"

"Just a little. They think anything can happen at any time. They believe the worst things. Honestly, it's very strange how protective they can be." She smiled.

Folding his arms over his chest, he stared back at her.

"Please, pretty please."

"Meeting the parents?"

"Yes." She touched his arm. "I'll give you anything you want."

Raising his brow, he nodded his head. He'd gladly meet her parents and put their minds at ease. "What do I get out of it?"

"What would you like?" she asked.

Wrapping an arm around her waist, he pulled her toward him, stroking through the crease of her ass. "This is what I want."

She let out a sigh. "That's it? Out of everything I can give you that's all you want?"

"What more is there?"

Jessica chuckled. "First, we've got a deal, and you can't back out now."

"I'm fine with that."

"You could have asked for a sex slave for the day? You, me, and a day where I give you everything, your every fantasy?"

The smile he had seconds before disappeared. He'd not even considered that.

"What?"

"Maybe next time you'll think about what you can have next time." She pulled away. "I'll see you after work?"

"Yes, I'll pick you up."

She wrapped her arms around him, dropping a kiss to his lips. "I'll see you soon."

He slapped her ass, watching her disappear back through the doors. It was still cold out, but it was no longer covered in snow and ice. It wouldn't be long before spring hit and they'd all be baking in the heat of the summer.

"So that's a real thing," Dime said, walking up to him.

"You better keep your dirty hands to yourself," Snake said, glaring at him.

"Don't worry. These hands are full of club whores begging for dick."

"They better be."

He watched Judi and Ripper leave in the car. The

Chaos Bleeds crew started to file out one by one.

"Are you helping with the selection at the strip club?"

"Yeah, we've got to start arranging for the talent."

"Does she know?"

He looked toward the hospital, shaking his head. "No, she doesn't." He wasn't interested in any of the women who were going to be working in the strip club.

"Devil wants us to start this weekend."

"Advertisements for the job have already gone out." Snake opened his car door, ready to head back to the strip club. "I'm going now if you want to jump in. I've got to make sure the decorators are doing their job."

"Devil doesn't want Lexie anywhere near this."

Naked Fantasies was the strip club's original name. They hadn't settled on a new one, but Lexie first met Devil while working in the strip club. Lexie's sister, Kayla, had given her Simon after a few weeks of him being born. In order to support him, Lexie didn't have a choice but to strip to earn a living.

"None of the old ladies are invited to the club." Snake turned the ignition over. "Dime, can I ask you a serious question?"

"Sure thing."

"Meeting the parents, that's a big thing right?"

"Depends. If the girl wants to dump you and to do it through her parents, then it's not a big deal. If she doesn't want to dump you but take things to the next level, then yeah, it's a big deal."

Snake frowned.

"Do you want to go to the next step with the nurse?"

He didn't say anything.

"Brother, you've got to be able to answer some of

these questions. You either want her, love her, or just want to fuck her. What's it going to be?"

Pulling out of the driving lot, he drove toward the strip club. The outside of the building held far more class than the original. It looked like a fancy bar and hotel rather than a strip club. When Devil and Vincent first set this bar up over ten years ago on the first trip into Piston County, they'd not given a lot of thought to what it was going to be like.

This time around, there was a lot of thought.

"Okay, do you like waking up with her?" Dime asked, drawing Snake back to the conversation.

"I like waking up with her and holding her. You better not tell any of the brothers this."

"Relax, Snake. I can keep a fucking secret or at least conversations of a more personal nature to myself."

Shaking his head, Snake blew out a breath as they both made their way inside. He seemed to be blowing out a lot of breaths lately. His life wasn't getting any easier.

"What about the sex?"

"The sex isn't the problem."

"You're not bored."

"No."

"Conversations?"

"We talk all the time. I enjoy talking to her. When she's not talking and silent, I want to know what she's thinking. To get inside her head."

"Dude, I think you need to face reality," Dime said.

"What reality?"

"You're in love with her."

****

Jessica ran toward the phone with a spoon in her hand. Snake had dropped her off at home an hour ago. He had to take care of things at the club, which she didn't mind. There was a lot for her to do. She'd cleaned her home, quickly before starting some dinner. With her parents and brother coming she wouldn't put it past them to drop in at a moment's notice.

"Hello," she said.

"Jess, is that you?"

"Lydia, you fucking bitch. You just upped and left me. I've been calling you every damned day and you're only now getting back in touch?" Jessica stopped long enough for her friend to start talking.

"I'm so sorry. I just wanted to drop you a line. Tell you that I'm doing fine."

"Fine?"

"Yeah. I, erm, I met someone."

"I remember you telling me that you'd met someone. Is it going well?"

"It's going great, Jess. You'd like him."

There was something off about Lydia. She was always so bubbly, and yet it sounded like she was close to tears.

"Lydia, what's wrong?"

"Nothing." She spoke very quickly, too quickly.

"I don't like this. If you're in some kind of trouble tell me. I'll come and help you. You know I care about you, honey."

"There's nothing going on. I was wondering about you. How are things going?" Lydia asked.

Glancing down at her tomato drenched spoon, Jessica fought the inner battle to tell her the truth or to lie.

"Actually, erm, I'm kind of dating someone." She gritted her teeth, panicking. Her heart was racing as she thought about Snake. She was cooking him dinner, and they weren't sort of dating. They were actually dating.

"Dating?"

"Yes, he's, damn, I'm so sorry about this, Lydia. It's Snake. I'm dating him. The guy from the MC club."

She bit her lip waiting for her to say something, anything.

"That's really good."

"You're not mad."

"No. I'm with someone else, remember? Be careful of Snake. He's not the staying kind of man."

Jessica laughed. "I know, but, erm, he's meeting my folks and my brother."

"He's meeting them all?"

"They're coming to town tomorrow. We're going to have dinner."

"I was wondering when you'd be free next, Jess."

She heard some scuffling in the background, and Lydia suddenly gasped down the line. Tightening her hand on the phone, Jessica's stomach twisted into knots. "I don't know when I'll be free next."

"I wanted to talk to you but alone."

"It'll have to be a couple of days. I don't really stay alone much right now. I've met another woman, June, at the club. We're getting pretty close."

"June's cool."

Someone knocked at the door.

"I've got to go, honey. I'll call you back soon, right?"

"Yes."

She was about to say something else when the phone was cut off. Frowning, she walked toward the door. Snake stood there holding a bouquet of roses. "I'm sorry I had to cut out on you before."

She smiled at the large display of red roses.

"They're beautiful."

Taking them from him, she handed him the wooden spoon. Walking back into the kitchen she couldn't stop thinking about the conversation she'd had on the phone with Lydia.

Filling up a vase, she listened to Snake talk in the background. She finished arranging the flowers, crying out as Snake put a hand on her shoulder.

"Whoa, baby, what's the matter?" he asked.

"Nothing, it's just—" She looked toward the phone.

"Baby, you can talk to me about anything."

"I've just been on the phone to Lydia."

He tensed up. "She phoned?"

"Yeah, she phoned, and she sounded strange."

"Did you tell her about us?"

Jessica nodded. "She didn't seem to mind at all. There was just something off about her." Rubbing at her temples, she tried to clear her mind, thinking about the flowers.

"Talk to me."

"Lydia's always so happy or talking a lot. This time, it was like she was being told what to say. No, I'm going out of my mind. This is what happens when you don't have a lot to do." She shrugged. "It's official. I'm going insane."

"You're not going insane." He tugged her close, holding the back of her neck.

She closed her eyes. "I just worry about her. I think I'm always going to worry about her."

"You might want to stir your sauce before it burns." He held up the spoon.

"Shit, thank you."

Rushing to the stove, she started to stir the tomato sauce.

"Do you want me to get one of the brothers to look into the guy she's dating?"

"Nah, I don't even know his name." She

shrugged. Jessica wasn't about to tell him the only thing she knew about this man was the name "Master". She'd not met him, and for all she knew, it was made up. "Did Judi and Ripper get settled in?"

"From what I was told, Paul hasn't been put down since he got to the clubhouse. There's always someone around to hold him." He chuckled.

"You better warn them it's not a good thing for them to keep holding him." She drained the pasta, before tipping it into the tomato sauce.

"They will. Devil was putting a ban on the holding when I went back to see them." She added the parmesan cheese before serving it up onto two plates.

Placing one in front of him, she took a seat. "What was with the flowers?"

"Can't a man do something good for his woman?"

She looked at him, forgetting about her concerns for Lydia. "It depends. Are they a gift or are they guilt?"

Snake stared at her for several seconds. "Today I was talking with one of my brothers, and something has been brought to my attention that I knew all along."

"What's that?"

"I'm in love with you."

She held the piece of pasta to her lips, staring at him. "What?"

"I don't expect you to say anything right away or even later on. I'm not expecting an answer, but I'm in love with you. From the first moment in the hospital when you wouldn't take any shit from me, I wanted you."

She touched his hand, trying to silence him. Words were failing her where once they were easy for her to say. "I can't talk right now. I really want to, and I have feelings for you as well."

"Jessica—"

"No, I believe I love you, too. It's too soon and sudden, but I do love you. I've never felt anything like this, but it's true." She pointed toward the phone. "I was willing to risk a good friendship to be with you. Lydia and I, we're good friends, but we're all over the place. If that makes any sense." She chuckled. "Like now, it has been a couple of months since I last heard from her, and she calls now, worrying me."

"I don't want to talk about Lydia. I want to talk about you and me." He took her hand. The food was forgotten. "There's no one else I want in the world, Jessica, and it scares me, too."

"I can't believe we're having this conversation."

"You're not the only one who feels like that. I've fucked a lot of women, and I didn't care about them. I used them. I don't want to use you, Jessica. I want to be your man. If you'll have me." He licked his lips, and her heart turned over.

"I've already got you." She got to her feet, moving to his side. He pushed the chair back, and she straddled his thighs. Wrapping her arms around his neck, she smiled down. "Does this make me your old lady?" she asked.

"No, I've got to fuck you in the ass before I can call you my woman."

She slapped him on the chest. He tugged her close, pressing his lips on hers. Closing her eyes, she wrapped her legs around his chair. She couldn't believe he loved her. It seemed so surreal, but she wasn't going to let him go, ever.

****

Master snapped the phone closed beside her ear. "When's she free?"

"In the next couple of days. Please, you don't

want or need her. You've got plenty of women." Lydia cried out as he slapped her across the face. The pain was instant, and she fell off the chair onto the floor. Grabbing her face, she stared up at the menacing man. He was supposed to be a charming businessman, and instead, he was a nightmare in reality.

"I've not got a woman that looks like her, and I want her. My supplier met with an unexpected death. I've got to find my own women."

She'd fallen right into his trap, never putting up a fight. He didn't want her to talk to him.

"Jessica is not like those women. She's not submissive or subservient. I promise you, you'll have a fight on your hands." She couldn't let her friend face this. It was all her fault.

She's got Snake. He'll protect her.

When she'd gone to the diner several months back, she'd seen the way he looked at Jessica.

Master took a breath, smiling. "I've always wanted a challenge."

He reached down, grabbing her hair, and tugging the length until she stood before him.

"I like a challenge, and this Jessica is going to be mine. You're going to get her to me."

"No, please don't ask me to do this."

"Chaos Bleed runs Piston County, and they've already taken my supplier from me. You're going to get me this girl."

She shook her head. He backhanded her, repeating his question. "You're going to get her for me."

"No, I can't." He slapped her across the face. She tumbled to the floor, gripping her face. He landed a blow to her stomach then another.

"You're going to bring Jessica to me."

She couldn't fight anymore. Shame hit her hard.

"Yes." Gasping out the word, she rolled over. He backed away.

"Good girl. It's about time you learned your place."

He walked out of the hotel room. Tears spilled from her eyes as the pain intensified. She couldn't let this happen to Jessica, and yet she couldn't think of a single thing to stop what was about to happen.

Chapter Ten

"Do you want us to go with you?" Spider asked.

Snake ignored the ribbing the club was giving him. He held Paul in his arms as the whole club was on babysitting duty. Judi was being tended to by the midwife to make sure the C-section wound was not infected or causing her any problems.

"I'm going to see her fucking parents, not to some war." He stared down at the little baby, and he knew in that instant that he wanted one.

"The brother and the father?" Pussy asked.

Across the room Pussy sat beside Sasha. The white cast on her arm didn't look very comfortable. The guilt whenever Pussy looked down at her arm was clear to see.

"I think it's good," Devil said. "We'll get to see what kind of balls the snake really has."

Shooting a glare at his Prez, Snake flipped him off while still holding Paul.

"Stop that, Devil. It's good for Snake to have found a woman he loves." Lexie walked into the clubhouse with Simon following behind her.

"When's Tabitha coming?"

"Soon," Lexie said. "Where are you going for dinner?"

"Some fancy hotel. They're staying at some hotel while they visit."

"It seems a little strange to me," Curse said. Mia slapped him on the arm. "There's nothing wrong with him meeting the parents."

"I'm not talking about Snake meeting the folks, I'm on about the fancy hotel. What's Jessica all about?"

"Her father's a lawyer and her brother a doctor or the other way around. I can't remember."

"Well at least none of them are going to come at you with shotguns demanding you marry their daughter or sister," Butler said.

"Will you lot stop this," Lexie said. "Anyone would think none of you have met family before."

"None of us have met family like Jessica's," Curse said. "I bet they threaten you by the end of the night. Lawyers have balls of steel."

"Doctors are the same," Mia said.

Rolling his eyes, he looked at the club that he considered his family. "You're not going to terrify me."

He was shitting himself. Jessica loved him, and now he was meeting her family. He was terrified of screwing up something that was in fact the best thing that had ever happened to him.

"You're all scaring him, stop it."

Judi, Ripper, and the midwife started walking downstairs. "Take it easy and have plenty of rest. There won't be any permanent damage, but the scar will be visible."

"I've no intention of going to the beach in a bikini, Ana."

The midwife smiled. "You'll be able to go to the beach one day. Take care." Ana turned to look at Lexie. "And you should be resting. That baby is going to pop out at any moment. You're going to need your strength."

"I'll see you out," Lexie said, chuckling. "What have I told you about talking like that in front of Devil?"

"He's got the right head on him that man."

Their voices faded away. Judi moved toward him. "Can I have him?"

"Sure. He's beautiful." Snake handed Paul back to his mother.

"Shouldn't you be leaving?" Judi asked, smiling up at him. He winced, thinking about the upcoming date.

"Are you scared already?"

"No, I'm not scared."

"I'm sure they're not man-eating parents, just concerned ones."

"You're all getting a laugh at my expense, and it's growing a little old." He glared at all of them. Feeling the back of his pockets, he made sure he had his wallet, keys, and cell phone. "I'm out. Take care."

He waved at them all, flipping several brothers the bird who shouted out names to him. Climbing into the car, he looked toward the clubhouse to find June sitting there smoking. She gave him a wave, and he smiled back at her.

Once on the road, his doubts started to fade away. Jessica was waiting for him outside. She gave him a wave, and he didn't bother to get out of the car. She wore a deep blue dress with plain black pumps.

"Thank you for this, Snake. I really appreciate it." She slid into the passenger side. Her hair was curled in ringlets down her body. She looked breathtaking.

"I wish we weren't about to meet your parents."

"They're not exactly excited about meeting you," she said. "I spoke to them a couple of hours ago."

"You've not told me their names."

She pointed ahead, and he followed the directions she gave him.

"My dad's William Stickler, my mom's Bethany, and my brother is Sean."

"William. Bethany. Sean. Got it. I'll remember the names."

"Don't be worried about this, Snake. It's nothing to worry about. They, erm, they already know who you are."

He didn't like the sound of that but wasn't about to worry over something he had no control over.

The hotel was fancy all right, and the valet stood waiting to take his car. Climbing out, he watched as Jessica ran around the car. She slipped her arm through his. "I want you to remember that it doesn't matter what happens here, I love you."

"I'm not going to take too much shit off them, Jess. I love you, and you're my woman. I'm not going to jump through any hoops."

"Just a warning, they're going to act all tough and make it hard for you. Please, try to keep your cool. They just want to unsettle you." She tightened her hand on his arm.

"Have a little faith." He cupped her cheek, kissing her lips.

They walked toward the restaurant.

"Hello, I'm under the reservation 'Stickler'," Jessica said.

The maître d' looked him over.

"He's with me."

Glancing around the room he saw he was the only one wearing jeans. He wasn't going to be dressed in a suit, not now, not ever.

"They're waiting for you, miss."

The man led the way through the restaurant. "Do you have a problem with my jeans?"

"No, your jeans are hot," she said, whispering the words back.

He spotted the table. Three people, two men and a woman sat together looking over the menu. There were two seats left.

They looked up the moment they approached the table.

"Hey, Mom and Dad," Jessica said. Snake waited while she gave each of her parents a kiss on the cheek.

"Not one for me?" her brother asked.

"I don't know where your cheek has been," she said, kissing his cheek anyway. "I want you all to meet Snake."

"We know him, Jessica," William said.

"It's nice to meet you all." He helped Jessica into her chair, glaring at the maître d' to back the fuck off. No one was going to touch his woman while he was present in the room. Once she was seated, he took a seat himself, staring at all three. William and Sean were glaring at him while Bethany smiled.

"I have to say I was shocked that Jessica was dating."

"He's a biker, Mom."

"Sean, shut it."

"He's not exactly the kind of man for you."

"This coming from the guy who dates supermodels with no brain cells. You're a doctor."

"So, I don't need a great conversation when I'm—"

He stopped, and Snake reached out to take Jessica's hand. He tried to offer her support as she faced her family.

"Be careful, Sean," William said.

"Please, William, don't start arguing. I know what you're all talking about. I'm not so delicate that I don't know what's going on. Our children are growing up."

"It still doesn't need to be a topic of conversation at the dinner table," William said, reaching for a napkin.

"You both are bringing it up." She turned back to him. "You're the first man Jessica has brought home in a long time."

"Mom, I'm twenty-nine, not twelve."

"You're my daughter, and you'll always be a little young to me." Bethany smiled at her. "You're a biker."

"Yes."

"What kind of club?" she asked.

He glanced at Jessica. "The MC kind."

"I have no idea what that means."

"It means they're bad men, Mom. They probably kill people and shit."

"Sean, stop it," Jessica said.

"What it means is that your sister, your daughter is protected. She will not go anywhere without me, and I'll make sure she's safe." He lifted Jessica's hand for them to see. "I love your daughter, and I intend to make sure she is well loved."

Bethany folded first. "Well, I can see you care about my daughter very much."

"I do."

"Dad, please, accept this."

"Do you love him?" William asked.

"Dad—"

"Sean, I'm talking to your sister. I don't need you to interfere and tell me how to speak to my daughter."

Snake liked William, but he wasn't too sure about the brother.

"Yes, I love him and I'm happy." She looked at the whole table. "I'm in love, and I'm happy. Can't you all accept that?"

William took a sip of his drink, taking his time before responding. "I'm not going to lie. It's hard to let you go, honey. You living in this town, working as a nurse, it's hard, but I will stop annoying you. If anything your club does puts my daughter in danger, I will find some way to end you."

"Dad!"

"It's fair, Jessica. I promise you, Jessica will never be harmed because of me." He smiled at his woman, his old lady. "I'll do whatever it takes to keep her safe."

He squeezed her hand to show his support.

"Right, that awful business is out of the way," Bethany said. "Let's eat."

"I'm not finished. I don't like him being near my sister."

"Sean, it's not your place, so back off," Jessica said.

"We can take this outside," Snake said. "I'm used to hitting with my fists. What about you? Do you need your hands? I can break them for you."

Jessica pressed her face into her hands. "Why couldn't I have a normal family?"

Silence fell around the table. "I'll leave it for now. I care about my sister. She's the youngest one, and we all care about her."

"I get that. You've got to realize there are other people who are caring about her now. I care about and love her. You're not going to change that."

"Fine."

They all nodded, accepting their places. Snake lifted his glass of water, toasting the Jessica's family. Reunions and dinners were going to be a blast. He would just bet the family had a lot of high flying members to entertain.

Taking a sip, he gave himself a pat on the back. He was going to make it through dinner.

****

"I can't believe you managed to get through dinner without killing any of my family," Jessica said. She closed the door behind Snake, smiling at him.

"I have to say your brother came close."

"He has always been like that. He's over protective and doesn't know when to stop being so." She hung her keys up by the door. Stepping close to him, she ran her hands up his chest.

"You're never trying to change me."

"What do you mean?" She frowned at him but didn't stop circling her arms around his neck.

"Some women would have made me wear a suit to meet the folks, but you didn't."

"So?"

"So, why not? Why aren't you trying to change me?"

She sighed. "If I got you to wear a suit now then you'd have to make up some story about who you are. When we saw my parents again, another story, and so on. I don't want to change you. I'm not with you to try to change you, Snake. I actually like you for you. I like you in jeans, and I like you out of them." She smiled, playing with the hair at the back of his neck. "I'm not one of those women who needs to be impressed or to impress their parents."

"You're changing my world."

"So are you." She went on her toes to press against his lips. It didn't take long for Snake to take over. He wrapped an arm around her, pulling her close. The hard length of his cock pressed against her stomach. She moaned as heat spilled from the lips of her sex. "I believe I owe you a little something." Pulling away from him, she took his hand and led the way up the stairs.

"I wish I'd taken the whole sex slave deal instead."

"Maybe you'll know for next time." She smiled at him but didn't stop her advance upstairs. Her heart was pounding as she walked into her bedroom. She'd found a sex shop at the mall in the city where she'd purchased the anal plug. It was enough to stretch her ready to take his cock tonight. She'd gone on her lunch break when he was busy.

"Before we do this there's something I've got to tell you," he said, halting her progress into the bedroom.

"What is it?"

"I'm helping the strip club reopen."

"Helping?"

"Employing women to strip on stage." Jessica paused not knowing what to do. "Before you throw everything out of proportion I want to tell you nothing has happened, and nothing is going to happen. I don't get hard for anyone but you. Will you trust me? I've got to do it for the club."

Staring up, Jessica frowned. She wanted to curse at him. "How long has this been going on?"

"A couple of days. I didn't want you to worry. We've not seen any girls yet, but that will change soon."

She didn't look away, and neither did he. "I trust you, Snake."

He cupped her face, drawing her close to him. His lips were on hers in the next second, and she gasped at the pleasure his lips gave her. Pulling away, she backed into her room. "I bought something for you."

"You're the answer to all my fucking dreams."

"Unzip me," she said, turning her back to him. He moved the zipper down, exposing her back. He unsnapped the bra she wore. She licked her lips as his touch ignited the passion inside her. "Get naked."

She left him to enter her small closet. There was a small mirror, and she took a small second to look at herself.

"You can do this." She whispered the words so that Snake couldn't hear her.

Removing her clothes, she bent down to the drawer at the bottom. Pulling out the anal kit, she looked around the door. Snake was naked on her bed.

"I'm ready for you, baby."

"I bought you a gift," she said, stepping around the door. Holding the bag on her finger, she climbed on the bed, handing it to him. "I think you'll like it."

He took the bag opening it.

"Are you sure about this?" he asked, seconds later.

"I'm more than sure. I'm ready. Aren't you?" She tilted her head to the side to look at him.

"I'm ready."

Snake reached out, sinking his hand into her hair. He pulled her close, pressing his lips against hers. She gasped, closing her eyes, and loving the feel of his mouth on hers. "You're my dream girl."

"I'd be careful. You've not gotten there yet." She laughed as he pressed her to the bed. His lips went from her lips down to her neck. Snake sucked on her pulse before going to her nipples. He kissed down her stomach ending at her pussy. Opening her thighs, she watched as he opened her pussy, licking and sucking her clit. Closing her eyes, she was so close to orgasm when he stopped, turning her over so that her ass rested on the bed.

"I'm going to play before I take this ass."

She heard the bag rustling as he looked through it. Glancing over her shoulder she didn't see what he was doing.

"I can't wait to fuck that sweet little ass of yours."

"I want you, Snake. I want to give you everything."

The rustling of the bag stopped. She couldn't make out any other sounds. "Press you butt up."

She did as he asked and cried out as his cool fingers smeared lubricant over the puckered hole of her anus. He didn't stick around to play.

"I'm just covering this plug. I'm going to fuck you with it, stretching you open, and then I'm going to fuck you."

Goosebumps erupted all over her flesh. Closing her eyes, she tried not to tense up as he pressed the slick tip of the plug against her ass. He worked it in slowly, taking his time as he pushed the tip passed her tight ring of muscles. Biting her lip, she dropped her head down to the pillow to contain her screams.

His free hand moved underneath her, stroking through her slit. Snake teased her clit, stroking over the nub, sliding his fingers up and down, and around.

She relaxed, taking more of the stiff plug. He kept up stroking her, feeding more of the plug into her ass. She cried out as he pressed the last inch inside her.

"You've taken it all, baby. You look so beautiful."

He stroked her clit as he started to fuck her with the plug. It didn't take long for her to start fucking back against him, taking as much of the plug as possible.

"I think that's enough. I want to be in this hot ass before you come."

She heard the tearing of a condom then some silence. There were no distinctive sounds to make out. Licking her lips, she panted for breath, waiting. She didn't have to wait long as the tip of him started to push past her muscles. The anal plug had opened her up enough that it didn't hurt for him to work his cock inside her. He was bigger and longer than the plug. He continued to stroke her clit, and it wasn't long before she was pressing her ass back against him, crying out.

"That's it, baby, fuck back to me, ride my dick."

Jessica was full. Her ass was on fire, and yet that fire only drove her crazy. She didn't want the fire or the burn to end. It was magical, electrical, and completely forbidden.

"My woman, my cunt, my ass, and my mouth. I own you all now, baby. No other man will know what you feel like."

"And I own that dick," she said, screaming as he plunged into her ass.

"Come, Jess. Let me hear those sweet screams."

He thrust into her ass, caressing her clit at the same time. The sensation was too much. She pushed back, moving herself onto his cock and fingers.

Fisting her hands into the blanket, she panted as the pleasure built to a fever pitch. She screamed his name as her release crashed over her. Snake picked up the pace, fucking her ass until finally he came, filling the condom he wore.

He collapsed over her, giving her all of his weight. She didn't mind. It was nice to be surrounded by him.

"Fuck, baby, you're the dream, the complete fucking dream." He kissed her shoulder, her neck, wrapping his arms around her before turning them to the side.

"Complete dream?"

"Yeah, you're my dream. My raven haired dream woman."

He tilted her head back, claiming her lips. His cock was still deep inside her ass.

There were times she couldn't believe she was in bed with Snake, the man she promised herself she'd never fall for.

"Marry me, Jessica."

Staring into his eyes, the scent of raunchy sex in the air, everything just felt right to her.

"Yes, I'll marry you."

Chapter Eleven

"You're getting married then," Dime asked.

It had been a week since Snake had proposed to Jessica. He'd bought her a ring and presented it to her at the club last Friday. It was now Monday, and he was sitting in the strip club waiting for the first women to come onto the stage.

"I'm getting married."

"There's no way I'm going to let any woman catch me."

"I thought that, and look at me. I'm going to be married. You have to admit that every brother who's married, is happy."

"I'm not going to be controlled by one pussy. I like the variety at the club. With you down, it just means more pussy for me."

Snake shrugged. "Don't care."

He sat back looking up at the stage. Music was turned on, and in the next moment a dyed blonde with fake tits walked on stage. "Hey, I'm Clara, and I'm here to rock your world." She pulled her hair down, grinding her hips to the beat of the music.

Watching the show, he couldn't help but look down at his cell phone. He missed Jessica already. After dropping her off at work, he'd come here. She knew what was happening today. His cell phone buzzed as Clara was getting to removing her shirt. He was pussy whipped, and it wasn't good for his image.

Jessica: How's the tits?

He smiled. This was his woman supporting him.

Snake: Not as good as yours.

Several seconds passed with nothing happening. When the phone started to ring, he let Dime know he was leaving to take a call. Stepping out into the fresh air, he answered her call. "Hey, babe."

"So you still like my tits?"

"I'll always love your tits. I'm a tit man." He leaned against the wall, pulling out a cigarette and lighting it. Most of the redecoration in the strip club was done now, and it was just down to the finishing touches.

"Really? I thought you were an ass man."

His cock filled with blood as he recalled the feel of her tight ass gripping him.

"What can I say? I'm a greedy bastard. I want both."

She chuckled. "I take it you can't come for lunch?"

"This is going to take up most of the day. I don't want to leave and prolong this shit."

"Come on, you're looking at women get naked. You've got to admit it's cool."

Snake shook his head. "I don't know what you've done to me, but the only girl I want is talking to me right now."

"You know all the good things to say."

"It's the truth. I know I can't spin you a line anymore. You wouldn't believe them." He inhaled on his cigarette, watching as three more women entered the club. They all had on high heels and barely any clothes. Jessica had ruined him. He understood what Devil and the other guys dealt with when it came to the pussy available to them. Not one of them appealed.

"I know. I'm going to miss you for lunch."

"Stay at work though. I don't want to worry about you heading home."

"Don't worry. I've not got anything else going on. Lydia's still off with her man, and she's not called me back."

"I'm sure she's fine."

He didn't want Lydia back in Jessica's life. Fucking that woman had been a big mistake.

"I know you don't approve, but she is my friend and I care about her."

"I care about you, Jess. I promised your family I'd keep you safe. We've been engaged a week, and if anything happened to you, they'd blame me."

She sighed. "I never knew how hot it was to have a possessive man looking after me."

"Fuck, yeah, I'm possessive."

"I'm not the one staring at dick all afternoon."

"No, you're the sexy hot nurse kissing all the booboos better. I don't know what's worse, staring at plastic tits or knowing you're making men feel better."

"I don't just take care of men. I take care of women, too. I'm not sexist."

"It's the men I'm concerned about, no one else." He finished his cigarette throwing it to the floor. Stubbing it out, he quickly checked the time. He'd been talking for the last five minutes.

"I can promise you there's nothing for you to be worried about. I'm all yours, Snake."

"Stay at the hospital. Don't leave it, and I'll see you later."

"Will do, love you."

"Love you, too," he said, hanging up.

Taking another breath of fresh air, he entered the strip club.

"She has you by the balls," Dime said.

"Whatever, man. I can't wait for the moment you settle down. You're going to fall just as hard as the rest of us. When you find the right woman, you're not going to know what hit you."

Dime burst out laughing. "Just keep telling yourself that, Snake."

Resting his cheek on his fist, he stared up at the stage. "Shut your fucking mouth. Tell me what's going on."

"Clara's hired. She's got an awesome show, and her tits are tight as fuck. It was a good job they'd done."

Snake wasn't interested in knowing what kind of tits Clara had. Another piece of music started up, and he sat watching a brunette strut her stuff along the stage.

Every now and then he checked his phone to see if Jessica had called. He didn't like this. Toward lunch the main door opened, and several of the brothers came through. He spotted Dick, Spider, Butler, and Guts entering the main club.

"We thought it was time to spread a little of the love," Spider said.

"No, he wanted to see what pussy he could fuck. June's on the rag," Dick said, taking a seat beside Snake.

"Dude, too much fucking information," Snake said. He didn't want to know about women's rags. The worst of it was Jessica was on hers. She'd started last night, and she'd gotten the worst kind of cramps. He'd lain behind her, rubbing her stomach until she fell asleep in his arms.

Moving away from Dime and the men, he walked up to the bar, grabbing himself a soda. They weren't stocked yet, but he'd brought something to drink.

"Are you okay, man?" Dick asked.

"Yeah, I'm fine."

He watched the men looking at the next women with interest. There just wasn't anything there for him to look forward to.

Sipping at his soda, he pulled out his cell phone to see there were no missed calls or texts. It was past lunchtime, and he'd be seeing his woman in a couple of hours.

"You're lucky, you know," Dick said.

"What?"

Dick wasn't known for being particularly nice to anyone, let alone telling anyone they were lucky.

"You've found a woman to put up with your ways."

"Dick, you don't even like people or women."

"I like women. I like a hell of a lot of things, Snake. No one cares to see what I like." Dick pointed at the men. "I'm not the only one that sees how wasteful this all is. The women, the whores, it'll all fade. What do we do when we're old with beer guts and we fart all the time?" Dick shook his head. "I don't know what we did, man, but this isn't going to be the way things are forever. We're getting older."

They both turned as Mia charged into the room. "Lexie's gone into labor. Devil's at the hospital. Vincent and Phoebe are there."

Snake charged for the door, not bothering to see who came and who didn't. He drove in the car, and he raced to get inside. For the last two births he'd been there, and he wasn't going to miss this one.

Jumping behind the wheel, he drove toward the hospital. Several of the men were on bikes. The parking lot was full, but Snake found a space to park. Rushing toward the reception area, he found Ripper and Judi waiting with their son.

"What happened?" Snake asked.

"She was cleaning the nursery, and her water broke. Simon screamed the house down shouting for Devil," Judi said. "I was there with Ripper."

"Was she okay?"

He looked behind him to see Vincent and Phoebe were sitting with all the kids. Phoebe was leaning her head against Vincent. The woman was starting to show signs of being pregnant again. Vincent was rubbing Phoebe's stomach while Simon walked around the kids playing on the floor as if he was the boss.

"Have you seen Jess?" he asked. He might as well see her while he was here.

Judi looked at Ripper. "I haven't seen her, have you?"

"No."

"It's okay. I'll just go look for her." He walked up to the reception and asked. They hadn't seen her either. Checking the time, he decided to go and check the cafeteria. There was no sign of Jessica but there was of Doctor Bastard.

"I've not done anything," he said.

"Calm down. Where's Jessica?"

"I was hoping you'd tell me that. I've not seen her since lunch. She got a call and left the hospital. I've not seen her since."

"Wait? What? No, I told her to stay here for fucking lunch."

"She didn't, and I watched her leave the hospital." Doctor Bastard shook his head. "She keeps leaving and not returning she's going to be out of a job."

"Fuck off." Snake walked away, typing her number into his cell phone. Walking down to the main reception he listened to the voicemail for a second time. "Will you keep me informed of Lex?" he asked Judi.

"Of course."

"What's going on?" Dick asked.

"I can't reach Jess. She's not answering her phone, and she left at lunch. I'm going to check her house." Something twisted in his gut. He didn't know why, but it did. Something bad had happened.

****

Lunchtime

Jessica made her way up to the cafeteria about to have the worst lunch in the world when her cell phone went off. Seeing it was Lydia's number she answered immediately.

"Hey, are you home yet?"

"Jess, I need you," Lydia said, sniffling.

"What's going on? What's happened?"

"I'm at your place. I used the key you keep under the mat. I really need to see you. I'm hurt, Jess. I'm hurt bad."

"Shit, fuck, yes, I'll be there. Stay there and I'll come to you." Closing her cell phone, she rushed past Milford. There was a taxi waiting in the parking lot. Rushing toward it she asked him if he could drive her home.

Within twenty minutes she was rushing inside her home. Her heart was pounding thinking the worst of what happened to Lydia. They were friends, and she didn't want anything to happen to her.

"Lydia, I'm here." Closing the door, she walked into the sitting room. Lydia was on the couch. She was bloody, bruised, and beaten. "Fuck, Lydia, what the hell happened to you?"

"I wish you hadn't come," Lydia said.

"What? You're not talking any sense." Pulling out her penlight she tried to shine the light in Lydia's eyes.

"Where's Snake?"

"He's working. Let me look at you. I should take you to the hospital. These cuts and bruises could signify internal bleeding." She winced seeing Lydia's wrists were also badly cut. "Who did this to you?"

Lydia opened her mouth, but it wasn't Lydia who spoke.

"She did this to herself."

Standing up, Jessica spun around to see a man in a business suit walking into her sitting room. He was buttoning up his jacket looking as if he owned the place. "I don't know who you are, but you need to leave," she said. Her hands started to shake as the noise behind her alerted her to more people in the house. Glancing behind her she saw two men in suits entering her house. Lydia whimpered.

"Yes, I think you'll do nicely. It has been a long time since I've had a woman with curves." He licked his lips, and Jessica knew she didn't want to ever know what he was thinking in that moment.

"You're not coming near me," she said.

"No? You're coming with us."

Lydia cried out, and when Jessica turned back to her friend, she saw one of the men held a knife against her throat. She gasped as the man she'd been speaking to grabbed her neck, hauling her back against him.

"I can have her killed with the snap of my fingers, Jess. My buddy there likes to run his blade across women's flesh and listen to them scream."

She couldn't do this.

"Lydia's outlived her usefulness, but if you come with me, I'll spare her."

"This is insane and crazy."

His hand went to her throat, tightening his hold. "What's it going to be?"

"Jess," Lydia said.

Staring at her friend she watched the man press the blade just a little harder into her flesh.

"Stop, I'll come with you." Her heart was pounding.

"Good. I always like it when people do as they're told. Bring the car around to the back."

"What should I call you?" she asked.

"You can call me Master."

Gritting her teeth, she tried not to think of the predicament she'd found herself in. Snake had told her to stay in the hospital and here she was with a man who'd threatened to kill her friend.

"Bring the car around the back. I'm not interested in being seen right now." Master didn't let her go. His lips moved to her ear. "I can't wait to play with you."

"You're not touching me."

He chuckled. "Honey, you're going to know every part of me." His other hand moved down her body to touch her nipples.

Closing her eyes, she tried to keep a hold of her senses. Her stomach was turning over, and the fear was getting too much. The man pressing a knife against Lydia's throat dragged her friend off the couch.

"Leave her alone. You said she'd be fine."

"I said she would be fine, yes, I didn't say she wouldn't be a little bruised before she got there."

She was propelled forward. He pushed her past her garden, and she was shocked that she did exactly what he said. She didn't want to go with him, but Lydia's life was in danger. Jessica didn't fight as Master gripped her neck leading her toward a blackened out car. The moment she got in there, she was lost. There was no doubt about it.

There was nothing for her to do. Sitting in the back of the car, she was shocked when Lydia wasn't sitting with them. "I thought it was only fitting that you come with me."

"Where's Lydia?"

"Up in the front with my men. They'll take us to my house safely."

Tears filled Jessica's eyes, and she looked out of the window to see nothing. There was no sign of anything clear.

"I don't want to be here. Please, let me and Lydia go."

"No, you see, Lydia's bored me, and I hate being bored."

"You've got to stop this," she said, biting her lip.

"My supply of girls has been cut off, Miss Stickler. I want what I want, and you're about to fill that void."

He let her go long enough to reach into his jacket pocket.

"What are you doing?" she asked.

"Don't worry, darling, this will only sting for a little."

He pressed a needle into her shoulder. Pulling away from him, Jessica felt her body start to grow heavy.

"What ... have ... you ..." Blackness filled the void inside her. There was nothing.

****

Gasping for breath, Jessica woke up staring at a plain white ceiling. Lydia, Master, the knife, Snake's orders, all of it came back to her instantly. She lay on a hard floor, and she rolled over trying to make sense of her surroundings. The nurse's scrubs she'd been in before were gone. She wore a long white gown.

"I have to say I was a little disappointed that our play will have to wait. I was looking forward to sinking my cock into your warm cunt."

She turned toward the noise to find Master fucking Lydia on the bed. Her friend had her eyes squeezed closed.

Revulsion struck her hard as she looked at her friend. Getting to her feet, she felt something on her leg. She couldn't move as there was a metal cuff around her ankle, keeping her locked in place.

Lydia was being attacked, and there was nothing she could do.

"I'm sorry that my menstrual cycle ruined your plans."

"It's okay. I'm a patient man, and you'll be all the sweeter for waiting."

"Snake will find me. He won't stop," she said.

Master grunted, and he pressed Lydia's face into the bedding.

"I know who the Chaos Bleeds are. They were the ones that not only killed my supplier but they're also housing one of my girls."

"One of your girls?" Lydia started to struggle. "Let her go. You're killing her!"

He held Lydia down a little longer before releasing her. "This one's a slut to the core. No one could tame her."

Lydia gasped, sliding to the floor and crying out.

"Brianna, she's one of my girls. You're all going to wear my mark." He tugged Lydia to the bed, spreading her thighs. "Look."

Jessica didn't want to look, but she knew she'd have to. Glancing down, she saw the burn on Lydia's thigh. "What is that?"

"It's my mark. I like my women to remember me always."

"It looks like a hot poker mark."

Master chuckled. The bedroom doors opened, and two men appeared. One of the men held a poker with a mark on the tip. It was glowing from the heat.

"What the hell?" There was nowhere for her to run. Master moved to her side, slamming Lydia into the wall when her friend tried to stop him.

"It's time to mark you."

The second man helped to hold her down. Jessica

screamed, fighting them off. It was useless. They pushed the shirt she was wearing out of the way, pressing the scalding tip to her thigh.

Her throat hurt from the screams. When it was done, she collapsed onto the floor. In the background she was aware of the noise around her. Her head was buzzing, and the pain was indescribable.

"Alone at last." She was lifted up off the floor. "I may not be able to fuck you, but I can play a little."

Chapter Twelve

Snake opened Jessica's front door and hesitated.

"What is it?" Dick asked.

"I know Jessica. She wouldn't leave her front door open." He pushed it open calling out her name. No one answered, not that he expected anyone to.

"Man, I don't like this."

He didn't either. Entering the house, he was pissed with himself for not having a weapon for this moment. There was no sign of Jessica. Entering the sitting room he glanced down to find her cell phone on the floor. He picked it up, scrolling through the last messages and calls.

"What is it?"

"Lydia, she called her last."

"Dial Lydia back," Dick said.

"I'm doing it."

The cell phone rang and rang.

"Hello," Lydia said, whispering.

"Lydia? Where's Jessica?" Snake stared at Dick while he waited for Lydia to answer.

"You need to help us."

He frowned. "Why are you whispering?"

"They tossed me into the bedroom with this cell phone. They didn't think I was going to use it. I was going to call you."

"Okay, I'm really confused right now. What's going on?"

"He has us, Snake. Master, he's got us locked in his home."

The name Master had him looking directly at Dick. "Tell me where you are."

She started to give directions to a secluded home out of town. He'd heard rumors that some billionaire owned the place and it was surrounded by metal security gates.

"What the fuck are you doing, you little cunt?"

Snake heard a man on the line. Lydia screamed, crying out, and the line went dead.

"We need to get back to the clubhouse."

The sound of a car screeching outside brought them both up short. He walked to the door to see who was making a dramatic entrance. Lydia had put his woman in danger. Fear gripped him. He didn't know what he was going to do if anything happened to his woman.

He recognized Sean as he rounded the car. "What the fuck was Lydia talking about?"

"Lydia?"

"She called me twenty minutes ago telling me she couldn't talk, but Jessica's in danger and it was all her fault. She hung up, and I tried calling her back. She wouldn't answer."

Someone must have been in the room when he tried to call back. Lydia was following orders, and answering the phone wasn't one of them. Fuck, Lydia was going to get them both killed.

"I know where they are." The problem was, he needed backup to get there. "I've got to go to the hospital."

"Why the hospital?"

"That's where Brianna and Death are. She knows who Master is." They rushed out of the house. Snake didn't make conversation on the way back to the hospital. There was no need. He saw several bikes in the parking lot, and among them was Death's bike. Charging toward the hospital he was aware of Dick and Sean at his heels. He didn't care what it took, only that he got his woman back.

Brianna sat with her head resting on Death's chest.

"What do you know about Master?" he asked, moving toward them.

Brianna tensed up.

"Snake, this isn't the time or the—"

"He's got Jessica. He's in town, and I need to know everything about him."

Death looked at Brianna. "You knew he was going to come to town?"

"No, I didn't. Gonzalez and Ronald are dead. His supplier of women is gone." Brianna pressed a hand to her mouth. "I don't know what he's capable of."

"What about Jessica? I need to know if there's anything I should be worried about."

"I don't know anything about him. He doesn't like staying in the same place." Brianna rubbed at her head. "We were always moving around. He's rich and can go anywhere he likes."

"So I've got a short time to get her back?"

"Yes. He's heavily armed. He'll have men with him who are capable of doing anything. They will kill anyone he orders."

Snake nodded. "I only needed to know if they were heavily armed."

"Why?" Sean asked.

He was already making his way out of the hospital. "I'm not going to put Jessica or the club in danger. I need weapons."

"Death, don't," Brianna said.

Glancing back he saw Death cupping Brianna's face. "I've got to do this."

Why hadn't he voted at the time to take out Master? Death had wanted to go looking, and they'd not long taken care of Gonzalez. Now this bastard man had

Jessica, and there was no hope for any of them.

"We need to get her back," Sean said.

"I'm going to take her back."

"This is your fault." Sean charged at him, slamming him against the hospital wall. "I told them you'd get her killed. You'd be the one to put her in danger."

Snake clocked him with his fist. "I'm not the one who caused this. I ordered Jessica to stay in the hospital. Lydia brought this to her. Lydia put her in danger. You want to blame anyone, you blame that little slut. Jessica was safe until she answered her call, and now I'm going to go and put right what she fucking fucked up." Pushing Sean away from him, he headed for the car. It was getting dark once again, and he hoped to God that he wasn't too late to save his woman.

****

Jessica stared at her bound hands. So much time had passed, it felt like years, but in truth it was only a few short hours, if not minutes.

"You're such a beautiful woman," he said, caressing his hand down her back.

She didn't flinch. Closing her eyes she thought about Snake, of his loving touch. She wasn't under any illusions. If Snake didn't get to her in time, this man was going to rape her, use her, and kill her. The only reason he hadn't raped her already was because of her menstrual cycle.

Last night Snake had held her, rubbing her stomach as the cramps had been painful. She'd hated being on her menstrual cycle last night whereas now she was more than thankful.

"I can't wait to show you off. You're going to be such a prize."

His hand landed on her covered ass. She wore a

pair of panties but nothing else. Her stomach rolled as he stroked her body as if it was his right.

"You're still convinced Snake's going to come."

It wasn't a question. She'd not spoken to him, and she wasn't going to start now.

"The Chaos Bleeds crew will never find you. They don't have a clue where you are."

He moved to sit before her. She stared into his eyes, trying to think of something, anything that would get him to leave.

The door banged open, interrupting him from speaking further and her from talking at all.

"What is the meaning of this?" Master asked.

Lydia was thrown to the floor.

"We've got to go, Sir. Your identity may be compromised."

"My identity is never compromised."

He stood up glaring at the men. Lydia cried out, and tears slipped out of Jessica's eyes. She hated hearing someone in pain, and this wasn't any easier for her.

"They're coming for her. We must leave immediately."

"I want her to come with me," Master said.

"We've not had the opportunity to make the arrangements. She has to stay. We've got enough room to take you."

Master didn't speak for several seconds.

"Chaos Bleeds. They're becoming the bane of my existence. Fine." Lydia cried out as Master grabbed her, dragging her against the wall. "I take it I've got you to thank for what happened."

"I'm sorry."

The sound of a gun going off made Jessica scream. She grabbed onto her ears to push out the noise. Lydia screamed.

"I wonder if they'll be back in time before you bleed out." He moved to the bed. "I'm so sorry little one. Maybe in time we'll be together again." Master lifted her up, placing her on the floor beside Lydia. She was naked, and she didn't even try to cover her body. He'd whipped and beaten her, using her as his own personal punching bag. "Such a waste."

He walked toward the door, glancing back at her. Closing her eyes, Jessica listened to Lydia crying out in pain.

"I tell you what. I'll give you this. Kill her when she gets too much." Opening her eyes, she saw Master put the gun on the floor. "After all, she gave you up without caring."

Then he was gone. She stared at the gun as Lydia gasped, and whimpered out. The pain on her thigh made it impossible for her to move. She found herself moving even as every inch of her skin was on fire, and burning. If both she and Lydia weren't taken care of soon, the wounds were going to get infected. She wondered if that was why he left her alive, either that or to leave her in fear of him coming back. Master liked to hurt and to cause pain.

"Jessica," Lydia said.

"Shut up." She crawled to the bed, grabbing her shirt, working it over her body so that most of her nakedness was covered. Grabbing the duvet, she dragged it over to them. Master had shot Lydia in the thigh. If he'd severed the femoral artery, Lydia didn't have long. She was bleeding badly but not enough to kill her.

Jessica had no strength, and she had no choice but to move around the room. Each step she took was painful, but she found a pair of tights. She didn't want to know why he owned tights. Collapsing to the floor, she did her best to bind up Lydia's leg.

"I'm so sorry."

"I don't want to hear it." Jessica tried to stop the bleeding, but it wasn't happening. Spots danced in front of her eyes.

"Snake called, Jessica. He's coming for you. I promise you, he's coming for you."

Once she tightened the makeshift tourniquet, Jessica collapsed beside Lydia's leg. It was too painful to move. Everything hurt, and she closed her eyes.

"Jessica?"

Squeezing them shut, she tried to ignore everything else. There was no way she could hear Snake's voice or movement heading closer to her. It was all in her imagination. She should have listened to him. The next time she was going to stay at the hospital. She wasn't going to believe what her mind was telling her. It was lies, all lies.

I should have listened to Snake.

"Jessica, they're coming. I promised you they were coming. They're coming."

She couldn't hold anything in. Turning to the side, she vomited, heaving up everything that she'd eaten that day. Being with Master she'd kept everything inside whereas now, she brought it all up, unable to keep anything down.

I'm going to die.

I love you, Snake.

I'm so sorry for letting you down.

"Fuck, man, she doesn't look good."

She recognized the voice but couldn't believe it.

"Jessica."

The darkness was so close. She just wanted to sleep. She was so tired. Tired and scared.

Sleep would make everything easier. Snake wouldn't be angry. She'd wake up to him holding her once again.

Chapter Thirteen

Snake stared down at his woman hooked up to several machines on the hospital bed. They were feeding antibiotics into her body to fight off any risk of infection. Her back had been cleaned and bandaged. Master, whatever the bastard's name was, had whipped her to the point that he'd drawn blood.

"I thought I'd come and check on you," Devil said.

While he'd been rescuing Jessica Lexie had given birth to a bouncing baby boy. Both mother and baby were doing well.

"She should wake up soon."

"Why did she pass out?"

"The doctor reckons exhaustion. She had an ordeal, and she just started to shut down." Snake ran a hand down his face. He'd charged into the room just as she was vomiting. Snake had caught her before she collapsed into the vomit. She passed out in his arms, and he'd not been able to wake her up.

"What about you? How are you holding up?"

"I'm here, boss. We've got to find out who this Master guy is. He almost killed my woman, and he's fucked with Brianna as well, then nearly killed Lydia."

"I've just come from seeing Lydia. I was shocked to see Dick sitting watching her."

"Both women had an ordeal." Snake stood as Jessica moaned.

"We'll talk about this in the club. I'll leave you with your woman." Devil tapped him on the back. "The club will back you whatever happens."

Going to the bed, he sat beside her, grabbing her hand.

"Snake?" Jessica said.

"I'm here, baby."

She opened her eyes, and he cupped her cheek. "I'm alive?"

"You're alive. You've still got to marry me."

Jessica smiled. "Did it really happen?"

"Yes."

"You came for me."

Cupping her face, he pressed a kiss to her lips. "When are you going to realize I'm always going to come for you? I love you."

"I love you, too."

"Your brother came with me. He's talking to your parents. They're dealing with your medical papers as I didn't have a clue. All three of them are in talks to try to make this hospital better," he said.

"My family comes from money, in case you didn't know. They'll be by to see me soon. I know they mean well."

Tears fell out of her eyes, and he hugged her close. "I love you so damned much."

Wrapping his arms around her, he let the tears fall. His woman was alive, she was well, and he was going to do everything in his power to keep her safe.

"What about Lydia?"

"She's alive. She's in the hospital. He missed her femoral artery. She's going to be walking around, fighting fit in no time."

Jessica pulled away. "I need to see her."

"No, not now. That bitch is the reason you're in this hospital now. I don't want you anywhere near her."

She touched his hand. "I need to see her. She didn't want me there, but she didn't have a choice, Snake."

He shook his head.

"Trust me."

Gritting his teeth, he nodded his head. "I'll see what I can do."

Leaving her room, he made his way toward the nurse. "Can I have a wheelchair? My woman wants to visit her friend."

"Sure."

He followed the nurse, taking the chair from her. Walking back to the room, he found Jessica sitting up staring down at her thigh. Brianna had a scar on her thigh, and she'd gotten it inked to cover it up.

"He marked me."

"Baby, we're going to take care of that. It doesn't matter." Jessica had peeled back the plaster and looked down at the raised skin.

"I can't believe he's marked me."

Taking her hand away, he rubbed the plaster around the scar.

"This is not who defines you." He took her wrist, kissing her pulse. "I love you, baby."

"He didn't break me, Snake."

"He better not have. You're strong, you're my woman, and I'm not going to let you fall. Do you understand me? You're not going to fall."

Holding her close, he helped her into the wheelchair. She wasn't crying. He took her down the long corridor toward the door. Dick was sitting in the chair, and Lydia was staring at the television.

"Jessica, you're okay. Thank God you're okay."

"Will you leave me a moment?" Jessica asked.

Snake didn't want to leave her but knew he didn't have a choice.

"Okay, but I'll be right outside."

Leaving her in the room, he stepped out with Dick following him. "It's good about the baby. Two more boys joined to the fold."

"I want to vote on this Master crap again. I want to find him, and I want to kill him."

"I'll vote yes," Dick said. "He needs to be stopped."

"Death will vote for it."

"After what we witnessed and what her brother witnessed, I'd say we're not the only one going to look for him."

He'd already talked with Sean after they got to the hospital. Sean was going to look into who owned the house. Snake had her brother on his side, and now all he needed was for the club to vote for him as well.

"I'm going to give Whizz a ring. We need all the help we can get."

****

"Jessica, I'm so sorry," Lydia said.

Holding her hand up, Jessica shook her head. "I don't want to hear you talk. You know, my eyes have been opened, and they should have been opened long before now."

Lydia whimpered. The sound grated on her nerves.

"If that had been me I would have lied my way out of it. I'd have told the asshole that I didn't know you, that there was no way to find you."

"Jess—"

"You didn't do that. You led him right to me and put my life in danger." Tears spilled out of her eyes. She stared at her friend and saw nothing. "We're done. Do you hear me? We're through. I'm not going to be there for you anymore. You're on your own."

"Jess, please, I'm really sorry."

"No. I don't want to listen to it anymore. From now on you stay away from me." She shouted for Snake.

"No, Jessica, please, don't leave me. I don't want

you to go."

She ignored Lydia, and Snake walked in. He didn't question her as he wheeled her back to her room. Lydia called out her name, and she ignored the call. Snake helped her back into bed, and she was so happy to be in her room.

"Are you sure about this?"

"She didn't even try to help me, Snake."

"Lydia answered the phone."

"She lured him back to my place. She put me in danger, and she didn't even warn me. I could have phoned you to let you know what was going on. Nothing." Tears fell from her eyes. He climbed onto the bed, wrapping his arms around her.

"I'm with you, baby. You know I don't care about the bitch. I never cared about the bitch. The only person I want is you."

He kissed her neck, and she turned into his arms.

"I love you, Snake."

"I'll protect you." He cupped her cheek. "I'm going to find him, and I'm going to kill him."

"I wouldn't expect anything less from you."

"You're not worried about what I'm going to do?"

"No, I want you to tell me when he's dead, Snake. I need to know." She touching his cheek, feeling the warmth of his skin seep through her fingers. "I love you."

"I love you, too, baby."

"Oh, honey," Bethany said, rushing into the room. Jessica was pulled into a hug that almost choked her. Looking over her mother's shoulder she saw her father and brother enter the room.

"Everything is taken care of. You'll have the best love and care here. When you're well, we're taking you home."

"No, you're not, Dad." She expected the threat of being taken back home. It was what her father always said when he found out she'd been hurt or in danger, even when she was a little girl.

"Jessica, you could have died."

"What happened today wasn't Snake's fault. It was Lydia's. I'm not leaving the man I love. We're going to get married."

William didn't look convinced.

"I'm not going anywhere, and if you try to make me, I'll never speak to you again. I mean that. You can't protect me from everything, Daddy. I know you want to, but you can't." She rested against Snake needing his warmth more than anything. "Snake loves me, and there's nothing you can say that is going to make me change my mind."

Her father hesitated for many minutes. He clearly wanted to say something else or get her to agree to go home. "There's nothing I can say?"

"Nothing. I'm going to be happy and married very soon. Be happy with me for that." She held onto Snake's hand tighter than ever before. He was the only person she'd ever loved and trusted. Over the past couple of weeks he'd proven to her over and over again that he wasn't the man she first thought he was. She wanted a future with him, to have children, grow old.

"It's okay, honey. We'll all get through this. Don't ever think I'd willingly let anything happen to you. I'm sorry, but when you've got kids of your own, Jess, you'll understand."

She smiled. "I already understand, Dad."

After a tense couple of minutes, they all sat down. Jessica was happy to finally be with her parents. She wasn't a fool though. She knew Master was still out there somewhere. He was going to come back whether she liked it or not. She shuddered, and Snake held her a little tighter for it. Even with Master out there, Snake was now alert, and no one was going to hurt her.

****

Lydia couldn't stop crying. She'd just lost the only friend who'd ever really given a shit about her.

Dick entered the room. He sat down on the chair beside the bed, staring at her. She was indebted to him. When Snake had entered the room, he'd caught Jessica before she fell in her own vomit. Snake, Death, and Sean had been there for Jessica. Dick, he'd been the one to help her while no one else cared.

"Did you hear?"

"It was kind of hard not to hear exactly what happened."

"She hates me."

"Yep."

"She'll never forgive me." Looking up, she saw Dick was staring right back at her. "You're not even going to say anything to make me feel better?"

"Why should I? You almost got her killed, not to mention yourself. Are you so desperate for attention you'll put yourself and your friend in danger?"

She didn't know him, and yet he'd know who she really was, looking past the wall she placed for others to see. "You don't know me."

"I know you. I know the kind of person you are. You've just lost your best friend for being a selfish, manipulative bitch. Grow up."

The tears she'd been trying to keep in started to fall. There was no way to stop them. "I know. Okay. I know what a shit friend I've been. Jessica has always been there for me, and I didn't give a shit. I'm a horrible, horrible person." She broke down, wishing her world could just end now.

She expected Dick to leave so she was surprised when he started to tap her back. "We all make mistakes. Some of us more than others."

"I can't go through life knowing she hates me."

"Then win her back, Lydia. Change for her."

Sobbing against Dick's chest, she didn't know how she was going to win her friend back, but she knew she was going to try.

Epilogue

Summer

"Is that normal?" Jessica asked, looking toward Simon. Tiny, Eva, and the family had brought the family to Piston County for the summer picnic. She watched as Simon sat beside Tabitha showing her some kind of playing cards. In the last few months she'd never seen Simon be so attentive to another girl. The moment Tabitha showed up, the love was clear for anyone to see.

Lexie and Judi were both sitting holding babies, and Eva was swollen with child.

"They're going to make for an interesting couple I think," Snake, her husband, said. They'd gotten married in April after they'd spent two months planning the big day. Leaning up against him, she smiled.

"Why?"

"They're from two different clubs. Devil and Tiny are being amicable for the kids. Simon helped Tabitha or something like that. I wasn't actually there to witness it." He played with strands of her hair, twirling them around his finger.

"You like playing with my hair, don't you?"

"Jess, my little bitch, I love everything about you." He cupped her cheek, tilting her head back so that he could kiss her deeply. She melted against him. It had been over six months since she'd been taken by the monster who'd marked her leg. She'd since had the scar turned into a beautiful rose on her thigh. It didn't matter how much she tried to forget about it; it wasn't possible.

Master was still out there somewhere. He could enter their lives at any moment. None of them knew who he was, but she had faith in Snake. He was going to find Master, and kill him.

"What is going on in that head of yours?" he

asked.

"Nothing. I'm just glad I married you."

She couldn't help but look toward the picnic table. Lydia was standing there talking with Dick. Ever since Lydia got out of the hospital she'd been with Dick. She was also trying to make it up to Jessica, but she wasn't interested.

"Do you think you'll ever forgive her?" Snake asked.

"No, I don't."

"Just keep telling yourself that, babe." Snake kissed her lips, plunging his tongue into her mouth.

This was why she could easily hate Lydia. Lydia had almost cost her the love of her life. Snake was the love of her life, her husband, and she didn't want to live in a world where he wasn't hers.

The End

www.samcrescent.com

BESTSELLING BBW ROMANCE
SPICY ROMANCE FOR REAL WOMEN

SAM CRESCENT

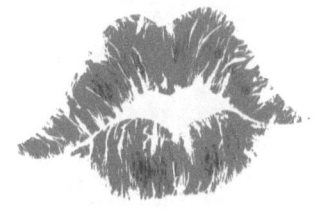

EVERNIGHT PUBLISHING ®

www.evernightpublishing.com